Enjoy the ~~~~
Wendy Trus~~~

Rose

MACGREGOR'S CURSE

a novel by Wendy B. Truscott

Loon Echo Publications

www.wendytruscott.com

www.facebook.com/hauntedjourney/

ISBN

978-0-9952108-5-1 (ebook)

978-0-9952108-4-4 (ebook)

Also issued in paperback format   978-0-9952108-3-7

Cover: Steven Novak www.novakillustration.com

Back cover sketch: Wendy B. Truscott

General Store, Muskoka Heritage Place

Story Editor: Ellen Besen

1 .Family Relationships 2. Youth 3. Loss of Parent

4 . Grief 5. History 6. Muskoka   7. Settlers 8. Pioneers

9. Bracebridge

DEDICATION

To my parents, Beatrice and James Lawson, who first
introduced me to the wonders of Muskoka and its history.
To those who faced the grueling hardships of attempting to
settle this beautiful but inhospitable land.
To the Indigenous peoples who so frequently and graciously
came to their aid, yet lost so much.

And to Paul, my most loving cheerleader.
If not for Muskoka, we would never have met.

*Although the world is full of
suffering,
it is also full of the
overcoming of it.*

~Helen Keller

It takes courage to grow up and become who you really are.

~ e.e.cummings

Chapter One

The Outsider

Jamie MacGregor was on a mission. Call it revenge. Call it justice. He didn't care about words. He needed to act. In the tiny village, the handful of cabins and sheds he surveyed lay as silent and deserted as a cemetery at midnight. The occasional drip of melting snow from their roofs provided the only sound, aside from his own breathing. No dogs barked. No wagon wheels creaked along the still frozen track. No farmers gossiped outside the general store. He noted its drawn window shades. The business was closed, a rare occurrence indicating the importance of the day.

Until recently, the surrounding trees had bowed low under the weight of heavy snow. A recent thaw had laid bare their branches, allowing him a clear view of the area. However, he would also be more visible. Moving forward, he avoided the muddy, main route and passed through a small woods. In the far distance, he noted an unusual shape rising along the riverbank, and the soft sound of rushing water identifying it as the new mill.

Emerging from the thick trees, he approached his planned destination from the rear. The imposing two storey, clapboard residence had always impressed him, as it stood in stark contrast to the simple log cabins most people occupied. After a few minutes surveillance, he was able to confirm the doctor was not seeing patients on this day. Instead, most of the villagers had already gathered inside, waiting for the special occasion to begin. He had come for the same event, but with a different purpose: he would wait alone on the outside.

In front of the house, a patient horse, hitched to a carriage, also waited. Close to a side window, Jamie spied a tree thick enough for his purpose. He approached it with stealth, keeping an eye on the horse, not wanting to spook it and alert others to his presence.

Reaching the safety of the tree, he flattened himself against it. He was grateful for its size and ideal location. With his height and broad shoulders, he'd be well hidden. Despite winter's chill, nervous sweat poured down his face, blurring his vision and stinging his eyes, but he didn't dare try to wipe it away. Even though he was sure he couldn't be seen, it wasn't worth risking someone ~~might~~ detecting the movement.

He held his breath and listened. A deep grunt and the scraping of wood on wood indicated someone pushing up the lower half of a stiff window, releasing a mixture of merry voices onto the still air.

At that happy sound, a white hot rage shook his body. What right did they all have to be so happy? But he couldn't afford to lose control now. He'd planned for so long and chosen his moment carefully. He would only have this one chance. He had to get it right.

The voices had stopped. His heart raced. He'd lost track of time. How long had he been standing there? Had he missed the moment? No! He couldn't. He had to do this. Leaning closer, as far as he dared without being seen, he strained to listen until at last a man's voice rang out, "I now pronounce you man and wife. You may kiss the bride."

Unclenching his fist, Jamie hefted the sizeable rock he'd been squeezing so hard his fingers ached, placed it in his slingshot, pulled back hard,...and let it fly! The shattering sound of the missile smashing through the glass at the top half of the window provided a fleeting moment of satisfaction before screams erupted inside.

He ducked back behind the tree as the familiar, red face of his neighbour, Jim Whylie, leaned out the window scanning the surrounding bushes. "Who's out there?" he shouted, shaking a fist. "By God, you'll pay for this, whoever you are! Bastard!

Quick! He only had a moment to crouch down and half-run, half-crawl into the bush and get as far away as he could before the others, now pouring out the front door, could spot him. He was fast on his feet and with a bit of a head start, he knew he could outrun any of the others. Even if one or two mounted up, he knew the paths and trails where a horse couldn't get through the underbrush.

*****

As most of the men rushed to give chase, their stunned wives and daughters gathered around the newlyweds.

"Who would do such a thing?"

"At a wedding!"

"Shocking!"

"Disgraceful!"

"No respect!"

Beatrice Lawson stared at the offending rock laying amongst shards of glittering glass on the dark carpet. She noticed strange, dark red splatters on some of the broken glass. In a strangely disoriented state of mind, she wondered how they got there.

"Oh, my dear. You're hurt!" Dr. Joseph Paul, her new husband, placed an arm around her trembling shoulders and guided her towards a small sofa. "You'd best sit down."

Her panicked eyes searched the room. "The children! Where are the children?"

"They're right here. Don't worry. They're fine. " he soothed her.

Before she could sit down, her two younger girls threw their arms around her, while Samantha, her eldest, clutched her mother's uninjured hand.

"Oh, Mama. Are you all right?" Worry lines creased Samantha's pale face.

"I'm fine. It's just a little cut. Truly." She tried to soothe her girls, hugging each one in turn. Then, casting a worried glance around the room, she asked, "Where's your brother? Where's Caleb?"

"He's gone with the others," Samantha replied. " They're after whoever broke the window."

"Oh, dear. He shouldn't have."

Heather Paul, the doctor's daughter, spoke up. "Please don't worry. I'm sure whoever did this is probably way ahead of them by now."

Beatrice was grateful for Heather's calm demeanour, so much like her father's.

Joseph Paul had removed a starched, white handkerchief from the pocket of his vest and applied it to his bride's finger to staunch the bleeding. "It appears you were the only one hurt, my dear, but this cut doesn't seem to be deep, thank goodness. And Heather's right; don't worry about Caleb. He knows how to take care of himself. "

"I hope so," she replied. At that moment, Samantha let out a gasp and stared, horrified, at her mother's blood-stained wedding dress, as if noticing it for the first time . Beatrice, too, regarded the lovely, deep blue, embroidered fabric, the finest cloth she'd been able to afford in years.

She'd put so much patient effort into sewing something lovely and suitable for this occasion, it would be a shame if the blood didn't come out. But it was, after all, just a dress. Her biggest concern was her children, and thank goodness, they had not been injured.

Samantha bit her lip, "Who could it be, Mama? Who would do such a thing?"

Chapter Two

A Secret Place

Caleb Lawson came to a halt, listening. Nothing but the nearby caw of a crow, and a light breeze rustling through the pines. No sounds of anyone thrashing through the bush. Whoever had been running ahead of him had either taken cover and was well-hidden, or they were long gone. Spotting fresh tracks and broken branches, he followed them for another ten minutes, until they ended at a stream. He ran up and down the bank a short distance in both directions, searching for more. Damn! Nothing.

Well, no good-for-nothing bastard was going to get away with spoiling his mother's wedding! Blinded by fury, he plunged straight into the icy stream without even thinking to remove his brand new boots or roll up his trousers specially bought for the wedding.

It was only as he reached the other side, soaking wet, teeth chattering, and exhaling clouds of frozen breath that he realized what he'd done. He groaned, not just with the extreme discomfort, but with knowing there'd be hell to pay when he went back. This was the first suit he'd ever owned in his entire life, and it was supposed to last for many years to come. And the boots! He slipped them off, held them upside down and watched the water pour out. They were the finest he'd ever worn. After a growth spurt, his late father's old boots and clothes no longer fit, and his mother had insisted on good quality, built to last. And now look how he'd repaid her.

Knowing he could soon freeze to the spot, Caleb struggled to pull off his heavy wool, soggy socks and began stomping around in the mud, flapping his arms in an attempt to get some warmth back into his shivering limbs. He screamed a stream of curses at the top of his lungs, knowing he couldn't continue searching; he had to get back to the house and get warm before it was too late. Besides, the others would be waiting for him. It was his mother's wedding day after all, and he couldn't spoil it any further.   Poor Ma! he thought. She's probably in shock. If I don't go back, it'll just make things worse.

Hurrying back along the path, still trembling and now almost numb with cold, Caleb felt increasing frustration at losing his quarry. A little further on, his ears picked up the lively sound of a fiddle playing a jig, and he increased his speed.

*****

Jamie watched Caleb, wearing that fine suit of clothes and boots, surveying the banks on the other side of the stream for footprints and was certain he'd turn back. No one would be crazy enough to ruin such an outfit by continuing to give chase. As someone who'd never worn anything but his brother's beat-up hand-me-downs, he couldn't believe his eyes when the idiot plunged through the freezing water without a moment's hesitation. Was he insane?

He must be pretty damn mad, he thought, shaking his head in disbelief at the sight of the wet and trembling figure stomping around for warmth and shouting curses at the sky. Jamie was pleased with the havoc he'd caused and felt more than a little smug, too. It was only by knowing where there were stepping stones in the stream that he'd been able to stay dry himself.

When the bedraggled figure turned back towards the wedding, slumped in a posture of defeat, Jamie allowed himself to relax. He didn't know Caleb. He'd only seen him around, but he didn't want to get into a confrontation with him right now. Not that he was a coward, but he'd heard the rumours. The kid had run away for a couple of years, and despite the fact he claimed he'd been up north working in a mine, some suggested he'd been in jail. Who cared where he was? Jamie didn't need the aggravation. He had his own problems. Lately, there'd been days when he thought about taking off himself. But where would he go?

As always, his first thought was he could go to his older brother, Robbie. How he missed him! He wasn't far away, a couple of miles, but he might as well be living on the moon for all Jamie saw of him these days. Robbie had always watched out for his younger brother, but now he had a wife and his own place to take care of. And Jamie suspected his new sister-in-law wouldn't be too pleased about taking him in. He turned away from the cave's hidden opening and kicked at the ground. Well, who needed her anyway?

Although the day was unusually mild for February, his hiding spot was damp and cold. He had no intention of leaving for a while, in case others were searching for him. He couldn't risk a fire, but he didn't mind. He liked it here. He'd found this cave back when he was about nine or ten, and he'd never told anyone about it. It was his special place, and he wanted to keep it that way. He figured it must have been a bear's den at some time, but he hadn't found any evidence bears used it now. Maybe his human smell lingered and scared them off.

He was careful never to leave any food around to attract animals, but he had hidden a few special items there, treasures he'd found while out exploring: some Indian arrowheads, a snake's skin that had been shed almost intact, an intricately patterned partridge feather, and the skull of a deer that wolves had probably brought down. They were a child's treasures. But he was no longer a child. He was sixteen, almost seventeen,- a man. And today, he had acted like a man. He'd had his revenge when he picked up his slingshot and smashed that window.

Jamie clenched his fists in anger and frustration. After all his careful preparations and the successful execution of his plan, he should be experiencing a tremendous sense of satisfaction. But he wasn't. He felt strangely let down. He couldn't understand it. He'd done the right thing, hadn't he? No one else was doing anything, so it was up to him. Maybe that rock wasn't enough. He might have to come up with something else. Something big! He curled up on the floor of the cave. Painful memories of the past flooded back and a tear slid down his cheek. So deep was his hurt he didn't attempt to hold it back.

Chapter Three

The New Family

Samantha repeated the question on everyone's mind. "Who would do such a horrible thing?"

"I don't know, dear. I can only think it's somebody's foolish idea of a prank."

"But that's crazy!" said Samantha, "No one throws rocks at a wedding!" She'd never attended a wedding before but was quite certain on this point of etiquette.

Her mother smiled, and with great tenderness, tucked a shock of unruly brown curls back under her Samantha's bonnet. She thought, once again, how much her eldest daughter resembled her late father, with the same colouring and attractive hazel eyes.

"I'm scared," Chantal, the youngest sister, cried. "Oh, Mama, maybe you shouldn't have got married!"

Beatrice chuckled and kissed the top of her youngest child's head. At seven, Chantal was the image of Samantha at that age, with the same untamed brown curls and those hazel eyes. Unlike her older sisters, Chantal had been too young to understand the stresses and hardships of the years following their father's sudden death. Indeed, her impish behaviour and often comical remarks had been a blessing in those dark times and continued to be.

Before Beatrice could respond, Briar, the practical and responsible middle sister spoke up, "Don't be silly! I'm glad Mama got married. Now we have a father to help look after us." She swiped at a stray wisp of her almost-white hair and focussed her intense blue eyes on her new step-father.

"And I promise I will, " he assured them all. "But now, we have work to do, starting with your mother's cut." The doctor turned to his daughter. "Heather, perhaps you could step in and keep the pressure on it for a minute."

"Of course." As Heather took her father's place, holding the white handkerchief on Beatrice's hand, Joseph looked at Chantal's and Briar's worried faces. "Maybe you two would like to help me get the ointment and bandages?" he asked.

Standing to the side, Samantha was pleased to see her sisters distracted by this errand and now turned her attention back to her mother and Heather. She thought about how odd it felt to have "Miss Paul", her school teacher, be her big sister. It would feel strange, indeed, to call her Heather. But stranger things than that had already happened today. Then she noticed something else strange- a flash of light coming from her mother's head. "What's that?"

"Oh, dear. There are bits of glass in your hair," Heather said. "Let me try to pick them out."

"Take care! I don't want you to get cut, dear."

As Heather gently moved her fingers through the thick, auburn tresses, she said. "Your hair is so pretty, Mrs. Lawson. I'll try not to mess it up. I love how you've put it up today."

"She's not Mrs. Lawson anymore," Samantha reminded her, as she took over applying pressure to her mother's hand. "She's Mrs. Dr. Paul!" That seemed strange too.

Heather blushed, "Of course. I'm sorry."

"It's all right, dear. Everything is new for all of us. Please call me Mother, if you like, or Beatrice. I would be happy with either."

"Thank you." Heather hugged her new stepmother. "I'll get it right the next time."

Her father smiled up at her, as he finished bandaging his new wife's finger, closely supervised by Chantal and Briar. All of them faced changes. Heather struggled with how to address her new step-mother, just as the three girls now struggled with the idea of calling her by her first name. This was just one of many small adjustments to be made. No doubt, there would be much larger ones along the way.

He and Beatrice had both been widowed, and each of their children had had to deal with the loss of a parent, sadly a not uncommon occurrence in this world. But they'd all get used to being a family. Looking around at them all, he didn't doubt they'd get there eventually.

*****

"No good trouble-maker got clean away," Jim Whylie announced, as he stomped back into the house.

Joseph Paul shook his head in frustration at this disappointing news. "I have no idea what this is all about, do you?

"Not a clue," the farmer fumed, pounding one fist on the dining room table.

"It's freezing in here," Mrs. Whylie shivered, turning to her husband, "Jim, can we get that window boarded up?" He nodded, and with two others in tow, went in search of tools and material to do the job.

"I'll get this glass swept up," she said.

"No, you won't. I'll do it," Heather said, jumping up . "I'll get the broom."

"Certainly not, my dear. This is your father's wedding day, and you'll just sit and enjoy it." She seemed to recall what had just happened and that perhaps "enjoy" wasn't quite the right word.

"That is, if you're still going to carry on." She appealed to the bride and groom, "There's an awful lot of food ready, if you still feel up to things. But goodness knows, we'll all understand, if you don't."

The groom, whose earlier infectious enthusiasm and smart new suit had drawn smiles and admiring comments, now looked concerned and doubtful. "I don't know… Do you feel up to carrying on, my dear? This has been quite a shock for you, and your hand must be hurting."

Beatrice looked at her family's glum faces and made her decision. "Of course, we'll carry on. Thank you, " she said to Mrs. Whylie and the others in the room. " We still have much to celebrate and be grateful for. I'm fine now, and no one else was hurt. That's all that matters."

"Good," Mrs. Whylie nodded her approval. " Come on, ladies, let's set out the food." Several women bustled out of the room, glad to have something useful to do.

"Where's Caleb?" his mother asked, scanning the now almost emptied room. "Didn't he come back with the others?"

"Apparently, he insisted on staying out there," said Andrew, the Whylies' son. "I don't think he's got a chance of catching him though. The dirty rotter had a good head start."

No one spoke for a moment. Most understood Andrew's frustration in his own inability to join the chase. In the past, he'd been fast on his feet and would have been the first out the door . Since a traumatic accident a few years earlier had damaged his back, however, he could no longer do most of the things he loved.

Wincing with pain from having stood too long, Andrew grabbed an available chair and eased himself onto it, just as his mother stepped back into the room.

"Here's your fiddle, son." She held up the instrument. "I'm sure we would all enjoy an uplifting tune right about now."

Chapter Four

Home Sweet Home

Jamie woke with a start. He thought he'd heard a noise. Maybe he'd dreamed it? No, there it was again! Scratching. Something was moving around in the cave! He held his breath, while his eyes adjusted to the dim light. He hadn't intended to fall asleep, and he didn't know how long he had been laying there, but a stiffness in his back told him it must have been a while. The light through the cave's opening had changed, too. It must be late afternoon. He could expect trouble when he got home. But for now, he had to identify that sound.

A flash of something brownish-red. Two glowing, yellow eyes peering in his direction. Bear! His chest constricted with fear. When he realized it was not a bear, but a fox, he released a long sigh of relief, yet remained wary. It was still a wild animal and therefore, unpredictable. As his eyes focussed, the creature continued to stare at him, then sauntered back out of the cave and on its way. Jamie knew foxes were curious by nature, and this one hadn't seemed afraid of him. He wondered if it considered his cave to be its own safe place, too.

*****

Jamie's pace slowed as he neared his home. These days he was more and more reluctant be there and took every opportunity he could to stay away. The day's unusual warmth had melted most of the remaining snow into puddles, and soon the clearing would be a vast sea of mud. The cabin looked forlorn, its logs worn to a dull grey, the porch step on a treacherous slant, ready to fall off. He noticed no smoke rising from the chimney. Something was wrong. Why was the fire out? Picking up his pace, he crossed the remaining space, leaping onto the small stoop.

The door, loose on its hinges, swung open. Stepping into the gloomy interior, he almost tripped over the body of his father, splayed out on the rough wood floor. Fear grasped his heart, even as the smell of alcohol overwhelmed him. Not again! As he bent down to check for signs of breathing, another foul smell assailed him, and he screwed up his nose in distaste. His father's worn flannel shirt was stained with what looked like vomit. Bits of food clung to his untidy beard. A sudden loud snort shook the body, followed by mumbled words he couldn't make out.

Frustrated and angry, Jamie shouted, "Da, wake up! Wake up!" The older man raised one eyelid, muttered, "Go away." and rolled away from his son.

The cabin was damp and cold. Tossing a rough, wool blanket over his father, he crossed over to the stove and stoked the few hot coals still glowing. He added a log, and as he knelt down to watch the fire catch and start to grow, thought about the situation. This had been happening more and more in recent weeks. His father had always been able to hold a few drinks, but now he was consuming much more. It was as if he couldn't handle his grief and wanted to spend his days passed out, so he didn't have to face the loss of his wife.

"What about me?" Jamie wanted to shout. "I'm still here. I miss her, too!" Even though it broke his heart to think of her, he often pictured her, smiling and asking about his day the way she always did. He imagined the aroma of her venison stew, almost moaning with longing to taste it one more time. In shocking contrast, today, his only greeting had been a drunken, "Go away."

Rising from the stove, which was now putting out a good heat, he went to the cupboard to see what there was to make a meal. All he found was half a loaf of stale bread and an almost-empty bag of oats. On closer look, something moved among those oats. Maggots! Jamie's face screwed up in disgust. He marched to the door and threw the offensive bag outside.

The sound of raspy snorts and pitiful moans caused him to turn around. He watched his father roll over, tossing off the blanket meant to keep him warm. Jamie strode over and grabbed him under both arms, hefting him to his feet with some difficulty. His father wasn't a big man, but in this state, he was a dead weight. He half-walked, half-dragged him towards the cot in a corner. "Lie down, Da," he said, as the man at first resisted him before falling heavily onto the mattress.

Chapter Five

MORE CAKE

"I'm not sure about this," the new bride shook her head. Her face, wrinkled with worry lines, revealed her hesitation and concern.

"We'll be fine, Mother," Caleb assured her. "It was just some kids up to no good. Nothing for you to worry about. They're long gone." Caleb didn't fully believe this but the last thing he wanted to do was spoil the newlyweds' honeymoon. Anyway, they'd certainly be fine for a few days.

Dr. Paul agreed. "He's right, Beatrice. Caleb and Heather will manage things quite well while we're away."

Family and guests gathered round the couple's carriage. Armon, hitched up for the journey, pawed the ground, waiting for Dr. Paul to take the reins. Sensing the air of excitement, he snorted and tossed his mane.

The newly-weds had planned a journey to Bracebridge for a few days, where they would shop for supplies and enjoy staying in a guest house where rumours reported the cook prepared excellent meals.

Heather spoke up. "Please don't worry. We'll be fine. Go and enjoy yourselves." She hugged her father and her step-mother, and stepped back, so Briar, Chantal, and Samantha could also give their mother one last hug. They were too shy to hug their new step-father, but he bent down to kiss each blushing little girl on the cheek.

Watching her father help his wife into the carriage, Heather noticed how tall and proud he stood, his soft, gray eyes shining with happiness. She thought he looked younger than he had for a long time and was pleased for him.

Beatrice settled herself on the seat, spreading a cozy bear skin over her lap. Her heavy, hooded cloak hid her abundant, auburn hair, but her delicate features and remarkable cornflower-blue eyes remained visible. Despite the fine lines and creases life had drawn on her forehead, Heather had to admit the woman was still beautiful.

Shouts of "Goodbye!" "Good luck!" and "Enjoy yourselves!" rose from the guests. The couple turned to wave at their family and friends, and with a flick of the reins from Dr. Paul, Armon stepped out. As the carriage lurched forward, the sudden movement dislodged something which fell off the rear with a loud clanging and rattling noise. When people realized what it was, they broke out in laughter. Chantal and Briar looked at each other and giggled. This was their secret doing. The old pots and tins they had gathered and tied onto the wedding carriage produced a glorious racket as they bounced along the road.

*****

The last of the guests had departed. The children stood quietly looking at each other, unsure what to do next. For each one, the situation was new and strange. The younger ones especially didn't seem to know what to do without a parent being present. Chantal's lips quivered, and the noisy sniff which followed, indicated tears on the way.

Sensing their mood, Heather teased, "There's still some of that delicious wedding cake, but I imagine you're all much too full to want any more."

"More cake?" Briar's eyes sparkled with anticipation.

"I won't say no," Caleb laughed. "After all, how often do we have cake?"

At the magic word, Chantal's threatening tears dried up. "I'm going to eat so much my tummy will burst!" she said, dancing back up the path to the door.

"No, you won't!" Samantha declared. "You'll be sick, and I don't want to have to clean up after you."

"I won't!" Chantal protested.

"Now, now," Heather laughed. "No fighting. This is a happy day, and now everyone else is gone, we can have our own little party."

She was used to handling a room full of schoolchildren, but this situation was different. The five of them were now family. She watched as they crowded around the table, excitedly waiting for her to slice the left-over wedding cake. Samantha removed her bonnet, Chantal wiped her hands on her new pinafore, Briar stifled a yawn, and Caleb gave her a little poke. "Don't fall asleep, little sister. You'll miss the cake," he teased. "But that's all right 'cause that means more for me!"

It was clear to Heather this was going to be a very busy family, but she decided she was going to enjoy being their big sister.

That evening, Chantal did indeed have a tummy ache. She moaned and moaned. "Serves you right!" Samantha chided her. Nevertheless, she boiled hot water to put in the ceramic bed warmer and held it against her little sister's stomach.

"You'd make a good nurse," Heather told Samantha.

Briar had fallen asleep sitting at the table, her chin resting on her chest. She was in danger of falling off her chair. May gently shook her shoulder. "Time for bed, sleepy head."

By the time the girls had climbed the stairs and slipped under their comforters, they were too tired from the excitement of the day to even talk. Within moments, each one had fallen asleep.

Caleb lay awake in bed, replaying the events of the day in his mind. No matter what he had told his mother, he was still furious about the rock through the window and frustrated he'd had to give up his pursuit of the scumbag who'd thrown it. He didn't believe it was just a prank. He feared something more serious was going on. Something dark and even hateful lay behind such a terrible intrusion on a wedding ceremony. But why? Who could dislike his mother, or Dr. Paul, so much they would want to spoil their special day? Or was someone else in that room the intended target? These were disturbing questions, and Caleb vowed not to give up until he had answers.

Chapter Six

The MacGregor Way

In the morning, the village woke to discover the few spring-like days they'd enjoyed were over. Soft snow blanketed bushes and buildings alike, revealing an assortment of contrasting shapes and sizes. An imaginative person might see the outline of a face in the shadows cast on a snowbank, or notice how a small tree with outstretched branches had taken on the shape of an angel in a white gown.

By afternoon, freezing drizzle iced the snowfall with a slippery sheen, making walking treacherous for all creatures. It was a day for staying inside, except for those who had farm animals to feed and milk.

Jamie fell twice on his way to the little shed where the family's few animals were housed and was glad he wasn't carrying the pail of slops for the pigs. He mucked out the horse's stall and placed fresh hay in the feeding trough. Next he swept out the pig pen, and fed the hens. He hoped the sun would come out long enough to melt some of the ice, before he had to feed the pigs.

This wasn't a day to spend outside exploring. He'd have to pass the time in the cabin with his father and his hangover. Since he wasn't looking forward to it, he took as long as he could with the animals, putting off returning to his dreary home as long as possible. Even though there were just the two of them now, the place felt overcrowded and confining. Maybe his father would sleep most of the day. While he wouldn't mind that so much, still, his shoulders sagged with discouragement, and a familiar ache filled his chest, a sad longing.

"I miss Ma!" Although no one was present to hear his words, he noticed the hens cocked their heads as if they were listening. Not for the first time, he wondered how much they understood of human speech. He wanted to tell them, tell anyone, how things had been so different before she died. They'd been a happy family. Da hardly ever drank, and Ma always made the best of things, no matter what.

In the past couple of years, with only the three of them in the house, maybe Ma had spoiled him a bit. He didn't mind admitting that. In fact, he'd enjoyed it. Who wouldn't? He was the last of her boys to be home, and she seemed to believe he'd soon be going off somewhere else, too, like his older brother had before settling down with Melinda. Instead, she was the one who went away. His fists clenched, and the ache in his chest increased.

His mind returned to the wedding. He still didn't feel as good about his successful shot with the rock as he'd thought he would.

But, at least he'd done something. He tried to show them. Nobody else had.

*****

Jamie managed to cross the clearing to the cabin without falling again, which did cheer him up a bit, and decided to tip-toe in, so as not to waken his father. Pausing a moment at the door, he became aware of a strong, smokey smell. Something was burning! Abandoning his plan to be quiet, he threw open the door and rushed inside.

"There you are!" His father's voice boomed, much too loud and jovial.

"What's burning?" he shouted. "Something's on fire!" Why wasn't his father concerned? Was he too drunk to smell it? In a panic, Jamie scanned the cabin and spied tendrils of smoke by the stove.

"Oh, aye," his father looked embarrassed. "I thought I'd make us a bit o' toast, but I didna' watch the fire close enough and everythin' got a wee bit scorched. But dinna worry. I'll cut up some more bread and try again. Sit yourself down, lad. There's tea. I didna' ruin that!"

Jamie didn't know what to say. He'd never seen his father preparing food before. That was always Ma's role. She would have shooed his father out of her way. Still, he did as he'd been told and pulled out a chair to sit down, all the while keeping a watchful eye on his father, who was attempting to remain upright and not stumble.

The second attempt at toast-making was successful, and the two sat at the table, slathering some of his mother's last batch of delicious blackberry jam on the still warm slices. Jamie wouldn't have believed stale bread could taste so good, but he was starving. He hadn't had any supper the night before.

They ate in silence. What was there to say, anyway? And while he had many questions, he didn't dare ask them. When are you going to stop drinking? What's going to happen to us now, without Ma? Why did she have to die? And the biggest question of all: Why aren't you angry? That was a mystery. It was as if his father didn't care what had been done to her.

Seeming to read his son's mind, his father sighed and shook his head. "I don't know what we're going to do without your ma, lad. There's no replacing her, that's for sure. But we'll do our best. After all, it's the MacGregor way."

"The MacGregor way". Jamie sighed. He'd heard that phrase all his damn life. Whenever things were bad, his Da would repeat this, as if it were a magic saying. It had started with his grandfather, whom he could still remember, a short, bent, man with deep wrinkles, a sparse beard, and sad eyes. Grandda's whole family had been forced out of the old country, Scotland, when the Highland Clearances took place.

Jamie remembered the old man's bitter description of starvation and cold, when thousands of families working the land for wealthy, mostly English, landowners had been cruelly evicted from their homes and forced to flee. The owners had decided the rocky Highlands were better suited for raising sheep than farming, and fortunes were being made in the wool trade.

"They were greedy, lad. Sheep were more important to them than people. They treated us worse than their bloody animals!" Sometimes the old man would spit on the ground, to indicate his complete loathing of those hateful, rich men.

Some landlords at least ensured their workers were moved to other districts where they could look for employment. But there weren't any jobs, especially for farmers in the cities, and families starved. A few owners offered to pay workers' fares on ships heading for countries like Canada, America, or Australia. But many more of them had been vicious, sending in brutal gangs to get rid of their people.

"Those thugs set fire to folks' poor, wee huts. Imagine, lad!" Grandda would recount. "And they killed any who tried to stand their ground." At this point, the old man always wiped away a tear.

Grandda's family were among the last to be uprooted from their home. They had taken the offered fare and set sail for what was called Upper Canada. In the stinking hold of the ship, fever broke out, claiming many lives, including three of Grandda's younger brothers, who were buried at sea. But the rest of the family survived the crossing and adapted to the new country.

Through their own hard labour, and the opportunities Canada offered, the MacGregors, like thousands of others, now owned their own land, poor as it might be. Where the family settled, in the area known as Muskoka, the land was as rocky and difficult to farm as the Highlands had been. But it felt familiar. It felt like home. They had survived the worst. It was the MacGregor way.

"This place is evra' bit as harsh as the old country, lad," Grandda used to acknowledge, "But the difference is here we're free men. No greedy bastards can drive us off our own land! Never forget that."

*****

Da broke into Jamie's thoughts. "Aye," he repeated softly. "We'll survive."

Jamie wondered if maybe there was a MacGregor curse. Members of the clan were supposed to be descended from royalty. That's what the Gaelic words on their crest meant. And they did have their heroes, like the famous Rob Roy MacGregor, who had valiantly fought the English king. But all that had brought them was having their name, MacGregor, banished when they ended up on the losing side. For generations, by royal decree, no one could call themselves a MacGregor on pain of death. They'd had to assume new names and hide their identity.

After all the soul-crushing events Jamie's own family had endured, banished from their home in Scotland, and Grandda's brothers dying at sea, they'd arrived here to discover the land they were to homestead almost useless for farming. It might all be theirs, free and clear, but it was still useless. Descended from royalty, Jamie scoffed. What a lousy joke!

And now, his ma was gone. What would be next? What if his da kept on drinking? What if he drank himself to death? And if he did, what would happen to him, Jamie? It all sure seemed like some kind of curse to him.

Chapter Seven

Finders Keepers

By late March, fickle Mother Nature was doing her best to warm up again. Soon the only patches of ice remaining were in the dense bush, where the sun couldn't penetrate. Open clearings were bare. The earth warmed and gave off intoxicating whiffs of spring, a heady combination of fall's decaying leaves, broken twigs torn from trees by winter's winds, wet patches from the sudden melt, and new growth struggling to burst through those layers of debris. The first raucous cawing of crows lifted winter-weary hearts.

Responding to spring's call, Jamie decided to take his slingshot out for target practice. He hadn't used it for several days, and for the first time, he noticed it wasn't in its usual place, hanging on a peg by the door. Strange!

His slingshot was a prized possession, made for him when he was little by his Grandda, who had carved not only Jamie's initials on it but a miniature version of the MacGregor crest as well. It didn't take long to search the entire cabin.

When he realized it wasn't there, he became frantic. Think! Think! Where could it be?

He tried to remember when he'd last used it. He'd shot at a black squirrel and missed. Good thing nobody saw that embarrassing moment. But that was over two weeks ago. He must have used it since then. Think, he repeated to himself. Then it hit him. The wedding! Could he have been dumb enough to lose it there? A dull, throbbing pain started in his head. Desperate, he searched the cabin again, knowing in his sinking heart he was wasting his time.

*****

"Ninety-nine! One hundred! Ready or not here I come!" May Whylie shouted. While her mother shopped for supplies at the general store and visited with Andrew, May was visiting Samantha. It was a fine Saturday, and the two older girls would have preferred to be exploring the woods, or sitting and talking. But with Samantha's mother still away, Heather had asked them to watch over Chantal and Briar.

At fourteen, May believed she was too grown up to play Hide and Seek, but she was happy to see the little girls enjoying themselves. Even Samantha was getting into the spirit of fun and taking the hiding part seriously. Setting off to find the children, May wondered what clever spot Samantha had found this time.

Chantal was usually the first to be found, but May certainly did not expect to see the little girl leave her hiding place and run towards her as she did now. "Look, everybody! Look what I found!" the excited child cried, jumping in circles and clutching something in her upraised fist. "It's mine to keep, isn't it? 'Finders keepers. Losers weepers."

"What is it?" Curiosity brought Briar out from her own hiding spot.

Samantha came running from the other side of the house, frowning. "What have you got, Chantal? Let me see. "

May realized her friend was worried her sister might have found something dangerous. "It's all right," she assured her. "It's just a slingshot."

"I can keep it, can't I? Remember? Finders keepers. Losers weepers?" Chantal held her found treasure behind her back, guarding it from the others.

"That depends," Samantha said. "If somebody says it's theirs, you'll have to give it back. Show it to me."

Chantal shook her head and took a step back. "Chantal..." Samantha stared her sister down until with a deep, reluctant sigh, the slingshot was handed over.

"There's something carved on it," May pointed out.

"Somebody's initials: 'J.M.'. Do we know anyone with those initials?"

"It has to be one of the boys," Briar stated. "Girls don't play with slingshots." She cast a disdainful look at Chantal.

"I don't care. I would play with it!" Chantal retorted, but now she sensed she might not be able to keep this particular one. "Stupid boys!" she muttered, kicking the ground.

Samantha stepped in. "Where exactly did you find it?"

When she examined the place Chantal indicated, she noticed how close it was to the house. Who had been around there? For reasons she couldn't explain, she became uneasy.

"There's no way of knowing how long it was there," May observed.

"It could have been Indians, a long, long, time ago!" Chantal's eyes shone with hope. "They won't be coming back for it, so it's mine."

"I don't know," Samantha said. "You could really hurt someone with this." She wasn't sure what to do, and with relief, remembered she didn't have to be the one to decide. "Mother will be home tomorrow. Let's let her decide."

Her little sister scowled but, for once, said nothing. To Samantha's relief, Briar came to the rescue. "Come on, Chantal. Let's go to the pond and look for tadpoles."

"Yay!" Chantal ran off, her attention now focussed elsewhere.

Shaking her head, Samantha confessed to May, "I'll be awfully glad when Mother is back!"

Chapter Eight

Evidence

Caleb hefted the slingshot in his hand. "It hasn't been out there long. It'd be more weathered and dirty."

"Something else is carved on it besides the initials," Samantha pointed out. "I didn't notice it at first, because it's on the other side. It looks like some kind of symbol, but I'm not sure. It's too tiny."

"I saw it, but it doesn't mean anything to me, either." He didn't want to alarm his sister so he kept his other thoughts to himself. With his parents away, he was concerned.

If it hadn't been there too long, and it was fairly close to the house, what could that mean? Had someone just passing by dropped it? Or had someone been lurking around, possibly watching the family? The hairs on the back of his neck prickled. People didn't usually walk that close to this house. It wasn't near any paths or trails.

Caleb rejected his first theory of a casual passer-by and returned to the second. He didn't like the idea someone had been watching his home. What would be the point? He rejected that idea, too. Then it struck him. The rock through the window! With mounting excitement, he tightened his grip on the slingshot. What if it belonged to whoever broke the window? He could almost picture it falling out of a back pocket when the culprit raced off. And who is J.M? he wondered, suddenly determined to find out.

*****

In the general store, Andrew Whylie was sweeping the floor, preparing to close, when Caleb Lawson walked in. In the past, Andrew had done his best to make Caleb's life miserable, because he was jealous his father had hired him to work on their farm. But after Caleb saved his sister, May's, life, Andrew had relented. An uneasy truce was established.

He still bore some resentment. Because of his accident, he was no longer capable of working alongside his father on the farm he loved, but he knew none of that was Caleb's fault. He was also truly grateful the fellow had been brave enough to save his sister from drowning in that raging creek. However, the two were still wary of each other.

Caleb closed the door behind him and nodded. Andrew nodded back but waited for Caleb to speak first.

"I thought you might know who this belongs to."

Andrew regarded the slingshot. "There's plenty of those around. Almost every kid has one."

"This one's different," Caleb indicated the initials. "J.M. They don't mean anything to me, but you see more people coming in and out of here all the time. I thought you might be able to help."

"Lots of families have names starting with 'M'."

Caleb stared him down. Andrew sighed and thought for a minute. "There's Allan MacDonald's family, and the Morrisons, and Millers," he paused. "And that's just for a start. But none of them have boys. The MacDonalds have three girls, and Morrisons don't have any kids yet." Seeing Caleb about to ask, he added, "And the Millers are quite old. They live alone over by my family."

"There's something else." Caleb pointed to the tiny symbol. "We don't know what this is. Do you?"

Andrew shook his head. "It's only a slingshot. Whoever lost it can easily make another one." He noticed the frustrated expression on Caleb's face. "Why's it so important?"

"We found it near the house. It means someone was there recently, maybe watching the place."

"Why would anybody be watching your place? Some kid lost it, that's all."

"Don't forget the rock through the window at the wedding."

"You think that's what did it! It was a pretty big rock!"

"Yeah, but it wouldn't be an impossible shot for someone who really knows how to use one of these. Or maybe they didn't use it. Maybe they threw the rock. Either way, whoever did it still could've dropped it. It might've fallen out of their pocket or something."

Andrew shook his head and resumed sweeping. "You're imagining things."

Caleb turned to go, frustrated and disappointed, but Andrew interrupted his thoughts. "Why don't you ask Dr.

Paul when he gets back? He knows a lot of people. More than I do."

"Thanks!" Caleb brightened. "Don't know why I didn't think of that." He smiled and left, feeling more hopeful.

Andrew shook his head. Finding the owner of that slingshot would be like looking for the proverbial needle in a haystack. Caleb was on a fool's mission, believing 'J.M.' would turn out to be whoever threw or shot the rock through Dr. Paul's window. Nevertheless, as he finished his chores, he couldn't help running a list of names through his mind: Matthews, Morans, Martins, MacGregors... Mrs. MacGregor had died recently, he recalled. It was too bad. She had been a friendly person anytime she and her husband had come into the store. As far as he knew, their sons were grown and married, and unlikely to be playing with slingshots.

Chapter Nine

Who is J.M.?

Several days later, Dr. Paul mused, "This little carved symbol is intriguing." He walked over to the window in his office to examine what he held in his hands in brighter light. "It seems familiar, as if I've seen it before, but I can't remember where."

Caleb had waited until the girls were in bed before bringing out the slingshot. Not wanting to worry his mother, he'd brought it to his step-father's office, where she wouldn't hear what they were discussing.

Now Dr. Paul and his mother were married, she and Samantha, Briar and Chantal had move into the doctor's larger home. With Heather there as well, that added up to six people. Caleb had decided that was a bit too crowded for him and asked if he could remain in the Lawson's home for a while. Their horse was stabled there, and he'd have their dog, Rascal, for company. This was a good plan. He would have his dinner with the family but walk back to his old home to spend the night.

All these new arrangements would take some getting used to, not only for him, but for everyone. However, Caleb believed the future looked much better for his mother and sisters than it had for several years. Dr. Paul was a good man.

The clinking of dishes and clanging of pans reached his ears, as his mother and Heather cleaned up from dinner. Still, he kept his voice down.

"Can you think of anyone with those initials?"

"Not at the moment, but I'll give it some thought. There could be several."

"It's got to be some kid. Grown men don't bother with them. Neither do girls."

"You're likely right," the doctor agreed.

"I'm going to keep asking around. Maybe I'll put the word out we found it. If I don't say where, the owner might come forward."

"He likely has no idea exactly where he lost it," Dr. Paul pointed out.

"That's true!" Caleb became excited. "So whoever it is shouldn't be afraid to say it's his."

"Hold on! You're jumping to a conclusion here, Caleb. You can't be sure the person who owns this slingshot is the one who threw that rock through the window. And even if he is, you can't prove anything."

Caleb was reluctant to admit it, but he knew his step-father was right.

"I know I can't prove anything, but that's not going to stop me from looking. I have a strange feeling about this.

*****

When he returned to work on the Whylie's farm later in the week, Caleb asked Mr. Whylie if he knew anyone with the initials J.M.

The man narrowed his eyes and gave him a suspicious look. "What in the devil do you want to know that for?"

Caleb became hopeful. Maybe Mr. Whyle knew something. Yet he decided to proceed with care. "I found something with those initials carved on it, that's all. I thought I could return it, if I knew who the owner might be."

Mr. Whylie grunted in his usual manner, saying nothing as he returned to spading his wife's vegetable garden. Either he didn't want to give Caleb a name, or he couldn't think of anyone. With Mr. Whylie, you never knew. The first day they'd met, Caleb had decided the man was a conundrum, a puzzle. He could never be sure how he would react to anything.

May Whylie, heading to the barn, had been close enough to overhear. "Are you talking about the slingshot? I was thinking about it. One of the girls at school is Jessica Moore. JM, see? Maybe it belongs to her. I could ask."

"Thanks, May. But I doubt this JM is a girl."

"It could be though, couldn't it?"

"I suppose so." It was obvious she was anxious to help, so he added, "I guess it wouldn't hurt to ask." He was reluctant to confide he suspected the owner of the slingshot had used it to break the window at his mother's wedding. He didn't want to upset May, and he certainly didn't want the word to spread. "Thanks for the suggestion." He grinned at her.

May's shy smile in return told him she was pleased she might have been helpful. Caleb was enjoying how pretty that smile was, when Mr. Whylie's voice startled him. "May, don't you have to get back to your chores?"

"Yes, father!" Blushing, the girl turned and moved off with some speed.

Caleb's eyes followed her. He was often struck by how much she resembled her brother, which could have presented a problem, given the strained relationship between Andrew and himself, and yet along with her dark hair and deep brown eyes, there was a new, appealing female softness to her.

"And you," Mr. Whylie's voice rose. "What're you standin' there moonin' about? You got work to do, too!"

"Yes, sir!" Caleb almost snapped to attention, picking up his spade and returning to the job at hand. He knew his cheeks were burning and wondered why all of a sudden he should be embarrassed for simply talking to May. They'd been friends for a couple of years and had always talked about anything and everything. The way Mr. Whylie was acting, you'd think something was wrong. "And I was not 'moonin'!" he grumbled to himself, shoving the spade into the earth much harder than necessary.

"Take it easy with that spade!" Mr. Whylie barked. "You break it, 'n' it'll come out o' your wages! Mark my words!"

"Yes, sir!" Caleb repeated, turning away to hide his smile. He knew the man's words were all bark and no bite.

Chapter Ten

A Real Nightmare

The nightmare was always the same: Jamie was being chased through the village by an angry group of women hurling enormous rocks that snapped his bones and smashed his teeth. Blood gushed from his mouth, and he put a hand up to catch his teeth as they fell out, one by one. He stumbled and, as the women gained on him, they all turned into brides dressed in white gowns, and instead of rocks, they pelted him with sling-shots. As he cried out for help, a blur of orange fur streaked across the road ahead of him. When the fox reached the other side, it stopped and looked back, drawing the women's attention. Like a pack of wolves, they veered off to chase it instead, leaving Jamie bruised, bleeding, and battered.

At this point he'd wake up, disoriented, and sweaty. When he realized he was alone and safe in his own room, enormous relief would sweep over him, and he'd allow himself to relax. This morning was no different.

A faint glow coming through his window promised the long night was over. His pulse slowed, but a chill set in, and he couldn't get warm. He wondered if the tormenting dreams were haunting him for smashing that window and causing mayhem. And he began to feel a sense of guilt, which angered him. Why should he feel guilty? If anyone should, it was the bastard responsible for his mother's death.

Interrupting the wedding had only been the beginning of Jamie's planned revenge. There would be more. He just couldn't figure out yet what form it would take.

The sky brightened into a rosy glow. There was no sign of snow, so he made a sudden decision. He had a desperate need to go into the village and find out what was happening. Had anyone seen him breaking the window? He didn't believe anyone could have seen enough of him to be certain of his identity, so he felt somewhat safe going in. He wondered if anyone was trying to find the guilty party. There's that word again, he thought. Guilty. He had to know where things stood. Without waking his father, he dressed and slipped out of the cabin.

*****

The previous fall, a blacksmith had set up in the village, just down the street from the store, close to the doctor's house. Although Jamie had rarely been to the village over the winter, he'd noticed both farmers and village men taking advantage of the heat from the shop's constant fire and open doors, to gather, smoke their pipes, and gossip. To Jamie, it was surprising the smithy, a tall, muscular man named Carr, seemed to have enough work to keep both him and his son occupied.

The shop with all its clanging noise and fascinating tools attracted the attention of most of the children, too. A cluster of them often gathered at the doors on their way home from school to watch a farm horse being shoed. Not all horses cooperated with the process, so the ingenious blacksmith, wearing his customary leather apron, put the leg he needed to work on into a sling operated by a pulley in the ceiling. With his back to the protesting, fidgety horse, he pulled the animal's leg between his knees, extracted the nails from the old, worn shoe, and then removed the shoe itself. Next, he filed the hoof. Despite appearances, the entire procedure was painless for the horse.

Choosing from the stock of iron shoes he'd forged himself, using the fire and his anvil, he'd nail on a new one. The sweating hulk of a man, the glowing fire, and the enormous, snorting and wild-eyed farm horses created a riveting scene.

This morning the shop's doors were already propped open allowing a view of the blazing fire inside. Partly hidden by one of the doors, the blacksmith's son stared at Jamie. Although he had his father's height, it only served to accentuate his scrawny frame. Jamie had seen him from a distance once or twice but didn't know him. Still, he acknowledged him with a nod. His reward was a formidable scowl.

"And a good day to you, too," Jamie remarked under his breath, as he turned away.

Noticing two wagons hitched in front of the general store, he turned in their direction. The wagons meant a couple of farmers were in for supplies, and Jamie knew nobody liked to gossip as much as farmers, when they got together. They'd sit around the pot-bellied stove for hours, discussing everything from crops to politics.

"Look at you, walkin' down the road like ya own it," a low voice taunted.

Jamie spun around. He hadn't heard the fellow sneak up on him. As he'd first noted, the blacksmith's son appeared to be about seventeen or eighteen. He was tall like his father, but there the similarity ended. Where the father was muscular, the son was all boney edges. The father had no need to groom his hair, for he was bald, but this one's matted blonde hair looked like it had never seen a comb.

Given the nature of his work as his father's apprentice, it wasn't surprising how filthy his overalls were. And it was impossible to guess what colour his shirt might once have been. All in all, the scruffy person who stood before him looked like someone who could use a good meal, and he smelled pretty damn ripe, too. Jamie almost felt sorry for him, but the sneering comment had put an end to any sympathy he might have had.

"What're you starin' at?" he challenged Jamie.

"Nothin'. What's your problem?" Jamie decided to give as good as he got.

"My problem? I don't have any problems, do you?" A blackened finger poked at Jamie's chest. "I'm just sayin', ya look like ya got a carrot stuck up where the sun don't shine." A grim chuckle followed. "Must be mighty uncomfortable walkin' around like that. No wonder ya can't smile."

"Oh, go… go jump in the lake," Jamie said, turning away, admitting his words sounded pretty feeble even to himself.

"Might just do that one o' these days. At least it'd be more fun than anythin' else happenin' in this hell-hole of a place."

Jamie kept walking. Over his shoulder, he spat out, "So, go someplace else, if you don't like it."

"Might just do that, too. But first I'm gonna have some fun around here."

Behind him, Jamie heard an unsettling laugh, but he kept on walking. What was wrong with the creep, and why was he following him?

Racing up the steps to the store, he entered and closed the door firmly behind him. An attached, tinkling bell announced his arrival, and the handful of people in the store turned to see who had come in.

Jamie pretended to look around the store at various supplies, as if he'd been sent on an errand. Andrew Whylie was too busy with other customers to ask if he needed help with anything. When the bell over the door chimed again, Jamie's head snapped in that direction. He'd been followed.

Before he could turn away, his harasser caught his eye and, smirking, sauntered over to where Jamie stood trying to ignore his presence.

"Shoppin', are we?" young Carr whispered behind Jamie's back. Jamie ignored him.

"Got any money on ya?"

"Get lost," Jamie snarled.

"You should try bein' a bit friendlier." As he spoke, Carr looked around at the various items on the shelves. Jamie watched his conniving face, wondering what he was plotting.

"So, one more time. Ya got any money?"

Jamie didn't want to answer, but he didn't want to attract attention, either. "What do you think?" he muttered.

"All right. No problem. 'Member what I said about havin' some fun? Well, when I see somethin' I want, like maybe that shirt over there," he said, pointing to a red flannel one on a nearby shelf. "I find a way to get it."

Jamie hadn't expected this. "You're gonna steal it?"

"Shut up! They'll hear you!" Carr hissed, giving him a threatening look.

"You're crazy!" Jamie whispered. "There's no way you'll get away with it!"

"Shut up, I said. Now that Whylie guy's lookin' this way. No, don't look at him, stupid! That'll get him over here for sure."

Jamie didn't want any part of this. Turning, he attempted to leave but wasn't fast enough. A quick, firm hand clamped onto his arm.

"Don't leave. The fun's just startin'."

Carr was clearly enjoying himself. "All right, forget the damn shirt," he laughed. "Maybe we should start with somethin' smaller. Somethin' easy, like maybe pushin' outhouses over. Nah, that's for little kids, and there's nothin' in it for me."

Jamie's frantic eyes darted around the room, praying for help and yet, at the same time, not wanting to attract attention.

"Got it!" Carr's eye's lit up, as a wicked smile creased his face. "Old lady Robertson bakes pies most Saturday mornin's. They sure make your mouth water. You can smell 'em all the way over to our place. Sure would like one of 'em all for myself. Bet you'd like one, too. Right?"

"Is there a problem, fellas?" Andrew Whylie's voice was laden with suspicion as he appeared behind them. He scrutinized their faces, looking from one to the other for clues, and expecting to hear an answer.

Carr dropped Jamie's arm and smiled at Andrew. "What makes you think there's a problem?" He gave Jamie a light punch on the arm. "Can't a couple o' pals have a conversation?"

"Sure. Except it didn't look like a conversation, that's all. So, unless you came in for something, maybe you two should move on."

"Not a very nice way to treat your customers! It's a wonder you stay in business."

Andrew didn't bother replying. He stood and stared the insolent fellow down. They waited to see who would blink first.

"Come on, pal," Carr said to Jamie, punching him lightly in the arm, "We don't need to take this. We'll take our business somewhere else."

"But I wasn't…" Jamie began to protest, but the stern look on Andrew's face told him he'd be wasting his breath.

The brief confrontation had finally attracted the attention of others in the store. Stunned, Jamie looked around and realized that, in their eyes, he was now mixed up with Carr and his schemes. There was nothing else to do but follow the jackass out of the store.

The moment they stepped outside, he began to yell, "You ass! Look what you did! Now everybody thinks I'm a crazy thief like you!"

To his utter disbelief, Carr was doubled over laughing. "So, what? Who cares what those losers think? We didn't take anythin' an' it was fun watchin' that stuck-up Whylie get all worked up. What a prig! Come on," he watched Jamie, waiting for a reaction. "Admit it. It was fun."

Speechless, Jamie realized the so-and-so was actually enjoying himself. Carr was strange and utterly unlike anyone he'd ever come across before, but what happened next was even stranger: Jamie found himself laughing. It began with a small, almost-embarrassed chuckle, then bubbled up through his whole body, until it reached a loud roar. And it felt good. No, it felt wonderful! He couldn't remember the last time he'd felt like laughing. Maybe this weird clown was onto something.

The next surprise was finding Carr's arm thrown across his shoulders, as if they were old pals. "I knew we'd get along. Say, what's yer name, anyways?"

"MacGregor. Jamie MacGregor."

"All right, Jamie MacGregor, how about some pie next Saturday?"

Jamie only hesitated for a fraction of a second. What the hell! Why not? He told himself he was entitled to some fun. Carr was right, this was a hell-hole of a place: one where a doctor could practically get away with murder and live happily ever after with his new wife and family, like in the fairy tales his ma used to tell him. It was also a place where he, Jamie, was left alone and miserable with no family who gave a damn about what happened to him.

"Why not?" he declared. "Meet ya here next Saturday morning."

Chapter Eleven

Robbie's Advice

The creaks and rattles of worn buggy springs bouncing over stony ground announced an arrival. Visitors were rare, especially those arriving by buggy, so Jamie and his father hurried outside, full of curiosity. When he saw who their visitor was, Jamie took off without a word, heading across the clearing towards the surrounding woods. He didn't look back, determined to get as far away as he could. No way was he going to stay and talk to that man!

"Here, lad! Where are you headin'?" his puzzled father called out. But Jamie ignored him. "Get back here!" The angry words pursued him.

Dr. Paul dropped the reins and climbed down. "G'd afternoon, Ian."

"Afternoon, Doctor."

As the two shook hands, the doctor's eyes followed the retreating figure. "Something up with Jamie? Not like him to leave without saying hello."

"I dunno." Ian MacGregor watched his fleeing son, still visible as he moved among the trees. Except for the evergreens, most were in their early budding stage and not yet thick with foliage. Tiny sprouts of vivid green dotted the coniferous branches. It occurred to him that, normally, this was a time of great rejoicing. Winter had ended, and it would soon be planting time. But there was no rejoicing this year. Not with his wife lying in the ground. This grim reality slapped him in the face yet again, and he turned to the doctor, who had been there at the end, when Sarah died.

"We don't talk much these days. Things have been pretty quiet around here, since his ma died, I guess." Straightening up, he asked, "Can I offer you a drink? What brings you by?" He led the way into the cabin, and the doctor followed.

"I had a call out this way and thought I'd see how you were doing. As you said, it's been a while since Sarah passed, and I know you'll be missing her."

"Aye, that I do. That I do. Evra' day. And I thank you for stoppin' in."

*****

Jamie walked and walked until he emerged from the woods at a clearing. Somehow he'd arrived at his brother's farm. Damn! He hadn't intended to come here, and much as he'd like to see Robbie, he wasn't in the mood to talk to him today. But he didn't want to go home, either. He hesitated, uncertain what to do. He needed a place to hide out for a while, until he could be sure it was safe to go home. He thought about his special cave, which wasn't too far away and decided to head for it.

"Jamie? Is that you?" Too late! Robbie had spied him.

"Yeah, it's me." He sighed with reluctance and started across the field. "Hi, Robbie."

His brother hurried towards him, concern on his face. Robbie's hard, wiry body resembled their father's and he moved with the same long, determined strides. But his ginger hair and kind nature were their mother's. Sometimes, this reminder made Jamie miss his ma even more. At other times, it kind of made him glad. In a way, a little bit of her lived on. Today, he experienced a mixture of both.

"Is somethin' wrong? Is it Da? Has somethin' happened to Da?"

"No! Da's fine. I'm fine. I was just out walkin'."

His brother's frown showed he wasn't sure this was true, but he didn't pursue it.

"Well, come on into the barn. I'm filing Blackie's hooves, or tryin' to. She's not makin' it easy for me. You can talk to me while I finish up." Robbie retraced his steps, and Jamie followed.

"She gettin' any easier to ride?"

"Not much. She's still pretty stubborn 'n ornery."

Jamie missed talking to his brother. The two of them had always been close, the best of friends. Really, most of the time they were each other's only friends. Ma used to say they were like two peas in a pod. That changed about a year ago, when Robbie married Melinda.

Now, she's always there, Jamie grumbled inwardly. Things weren't the same. He wasn't comfortable talking about some things in front of her. Although Melinda was quiet and almost shy, she'd been friendly enough in the beginning, but lately she seemed to have changed. He had the impression she disliked him now, and he wasn't sure why.

The body heat of the few animals crowded together in pens warmed the barn. This familiar coziness, combined with the mingled odours of the creatures, fresh manure, and the crunch of straw under his feet soothed him.

"When did you get new piglets?" he asked, picking one up and rubbing its belly. The animal squealed and snorted with pleasure, its snub nose poking at his chest, as if asking for more. Two others sniffed and poked at his ankles, deciding whether he was friend or foe.

"Almost a month ago now." Robbie picked up one of Blackie's hooves. The agitated horse backed up, nearly knocking him over. "Easy there," he said, trying to calm her, so he could resume filing.

"I guess it's that long since you were here." He glanced at Jamie, waiting for an explanation. Jamie had been in the habit of walking over often, but his brother was right. It had been at least a month.

He had a sudden longing to share his fears about the blacksmith's son and his frightening threats with Robbie. However, that would mean revealing he was the one who'd spoiled the wedding, and he didn't think he could face his brother's inevitable disappointment.

Instead, he shrugged his shoulders and, without looking at Robbie, admitted, "Dr. Paul came by. I decided to come here."

Robbie dropped Blackie's hoof and straightened up, stretching his back a bit. "Are you still goin' on about that?" He shook his head in annoyance. "You've got to let it go. He's not responsible. The man did everything he could for Ma, but she was far too sick by the time we sent for him." He sighed, "I wish she'd told us sooner how bad she felt. But she kept it to herself, not wantin' to worry us, I guess."

The last thing Jamie wanted was a lecture. He glared at his brother and opened his mouth to argue, but Robbie warned him. "Let it go!"

The brothers stared each other down, each one as stubborn as the other. "Besides, the doc's had his share o' trouble lately, too," Robbie added, turning back to his filing job. "He doesn't need any more."

"What d'you mean?"

"I heard some crackpot pulled a dirty trick at his wedding. Smashed a window with a rock. Scared everyone half to death."

Hearing these words spoken aloud shook Jamie up, especially here and now, and coming from his brother. He felt trapped, not knowing how to act or what to say. A few moments ago, he'd actually considered unburdening himself to Robbie; now, he again feared giving himself away. After working up his courage, he asked, "Who was it?"

"Nobody knows. Some idiot, that's for sure!"

He should have been relieved no one knew; instead, Robbie's disdain deepened his fear of being discovered. He didn't think his brother would ever forgive him, if he found out.

"Ouch!" he yelled, dropping the piglet, who wiggled to his feet and, squealing, scampered away to join his siblings. "He bit me! I'm bleeding!"

Robbie laughed. "He was just tryin' to suck on your finger. Maybe he misses his ma, too!"

Jamie stuck his throbbing finger in his mouth. There wasn't much blood, but still, it hurt. He gave his brother a dark look. He didn't find any of this funny, especially the remark about missing his ma. In fact, wasn't he being compared to a pig? His dark look deepened. Now he was fighting mad.

Sensing his young brother's rising anger, Robbie placed a gentle hand on Jamie's shoulder and tried to make up for the comment. "It's almost supper time. You're welcome to stay. After I finish up here, we'll go and check what's on the stove. Melinda isn't a very good cook, but she's improving. And I'm guessing it's a lot better than what you or Da are eating these days. She can clean up that finger for you, too."

Jamie didn't want to see his sister-in-law any more than he wanted to see Dr. Paul, but given the choice, he decided to take his chances on Melinda's cooking.

*****

As they approached the cabin, the unmistakeable aroma of homemade bread flooded him with memories of his ma's cooking.

"Look who's here," Robbie's cheerful voice called out to his wife, as he opened the door to their cabin. "A stranger dropped by. I invited him to stay and have a bite with us."

"A stranger? You never...." Melinda turned an expectant face towards the door, but when she spied Jamie, her expression transformed into a scowl of disappointment.

"Oh,...It's you," she added, making no effort to hide her true feelings.

"Hi, Melinda." For Robbie's sake, Jamie decided to be polite despite her attitude towards him. "How are you?"

"Not so bad, thank you. But not so good, either." She rested a hand on her stomach and looked down. Following her glance, Jamie noticed she had gained a bit of weight. She tucked a wayward strand of hair back into place. Her fair hair and complexion always gave her a light, almost fragile, air, but today he noticed she appeared alarmingly pale, almost white.

"Go and wash up first, Rob," she said. "Your supper's ready."

"Yes, mother!" Rob laughed good-naturedly and turned to Jamie. "We'd better do as she says. She's pretty bossy these days."

The icy water in the bucket outside the door made him gasp, but Jamie dutifully washed his hands and wiped them dry on his trousers. The bleeding had stopped where the pig had bitten him, but the cut still stung.

"Melinda's a bit cranky these days," Robbie sighed. "You'll have to forgive her. She's not been feelin' well lately."

Alarmed, Jamie asked, "Is she sick?" He thought of her pale face, so like his mother's had been when she was ill. What would Robbie do if Melinda died, too?

"Nah, she's not sick, just a little queasy now and then." Robbie's grin stretched wide and his eyes danced. "There's a baby comin'!"

"A baby?" Jamie dropped down onto a nearby stump, stunned by the news. But why should I be? he thought. Isn't this the usual way of things?

"That's right," Rob laughed, landing a light punch on Jamie's shoulder. "You're gonna be an uncle, Jamie me boy! What d' you think of that?"

An uncle! He hadn't thought of that. What does it mean, to be an uncle, he wondered. He never knew his own uncles. They were far away. Besides, didn't you have to be an old man to be an uncle? He had a scary thought. Will he have to do anything special? Like, did he have to take the kid fishing when he got older, or teach him to hunt? No, that was his da's job. So, what does an uncle do?

Robbie was still beaming at him and obviously waiting for some kind of response. "That's great! Congratulations. Anxious to please his brother, he added, "Maybe I could teach him how to fish or hunt or somethin'."

"Sure! If it's a boy. But it might be a girl. I suppose girls could learn those things, too."

A girl! What the heck did he know about little girls?

"Don't look so shocked. It could be a little girl. And if it is, maybe we'll name her Sarah, after Ma." Robbie looked wistful. "Come on, Uncle Jamie," he said, brightening. "Let's go eat!"

Chapter Twelve

Anger Boils Over

It was dark when Jamie left his brother's house, but the three-quarter moon shone through the bare limbs of the surrounding woods, lighting his path. He followed the road instead of stumbling through the bush, as he had when he'd rushed off earlier to avoid Dr. Paul.

He breathed in the musky scent of dank earth, the scent of renewed growth. New life. This was the time of year his ma had always loved best. After long, dark, bitter months of winter, cooped up in the cabin, with supplies running low. it made her heart happy to spy tiny tips of green poking through the earth and trees bursting into buds. And now a new baby. She would have loved this, too. These thoughts renewed his familiar sadness, but now, beneath it, something else stirred. Was it a flicker of hope? He wasn't sure, but maybe.

Tiny creatures rustled through the dry underbrush, the clear night air amplifying their scurrying footsteps, so that a nervous person might imagine they were larger, wild animals to be feared. Alone with his thoughts, he had time to contemplate Robbie and Melinda's news and a great deal more. His belly was pleasantly full. He had stuffed himself with that bread fresh from the oven. And the soup had been surprisingly tasty, too. In fact, as he thought about the meal, he realized how much he'd enjoyed sitting at the table in the cozy cabin with his brother, and yes, even Melinda.

There had been that one moment before dinner when he thought everything was going downhill again. Robbie had gone over to the stove where Melinda was stirring a pot. "If you've got a moment, maybe you could have a look at Jamie's finger before we eat."

"What's the matter with him now," she'd asked with a sigh, as if it was just one thing after another.

"Don't worry about it," Jamie replied, instinctively putting his hands behind his back. "It's just a little thing."

"Show her," Robbie ordered. "Sometimes little things turn into big things. It needs to be cleaned up, at least."

Melinda reached for Jamie's hand, yanking it from behind his back. "Let me look. What happened?"

As he tried to explain, Robbie interrupted to repeat his joke about the piglet thinking Jamie was his mother and trying to suck on his finger.

"Robbie, that's disgusting." Melinda said, dropping Jamie's hand. "I'll put some salve on it. That's all I can do."

When her back was turned, Robbie winked at Jamie. "I thought it was funny. Too bad neither of you did."

Melinda returned from the other room and slapped on the salve, causing Jamie to flinch. "It can't hurt that much," she'd scolded him. "The cut's so small you can hardly see it."

Clearly, in her opinion, he was acting like a big baby. He wondered if she was going to be as uncaring with her own child. If so, he already pitied the poor thing that wasn't even born yet.

Robbie's scowls had made clear he wasn't happy with Melinda's attitude towards Jamie. As always, though, he tried humour before anger. "Yes, that little piggie sure mistook you for its mama. Can't imagine how, unless my little brother hasn't washed for a few days. Let me take a sniff and see." Dropping down on all fours, he made a pretence of sniffing around Jamie and making "oink-oink" noises until both Melinda and Jamie had no choice but to laugh.

Melinda got Robbie's message and later on, made an effort to be a bit more pleasant. However, Jamie remained bewildered by her attitude towards him.

He remembered how Robbie had declared whoever broke the window at the doctor's wedding must be a crackpot and an idiot, Jamie knew there was no way he wanted anyone to find out he was responsible, and if he was careful, no one ever would.

Absorbed in these thoughts, he hadn't remained aware of his surrounding, until a tingling sixth sense brought him to an abrupt halt. With wary eyes, he scanned the surrounding darkness on both sides of the road, and then he saw it. Moonlight reflected off a pair of yellow eyes set in a head cocked to one side in an inquisitive manner, as if sizing him up. Jamie and the young fox studied each other for several seconds, before the creature widened its mouth showing razor-edged teeth. As Jamie stiffened, uncertain what to do, the fox simply yawned in a relaxed fashion, shook its furry, red coat, and with another quizzical look at him, turned and melted back into the thick blackness of the bush.

What was that all about? he wondered. The animal had seemed almost friendly. Could it be the same one he'd seen in his cave?

A strange sense of magic filled the silence where he walked now, almost as if he were the only living person in the whole world. However, instead of the loneliness he might have expected, for the first time in a long while, a calmness settled in his soul.

*****

As his own home came into view, he was struck by how forlorn it looked. A dim light shone within, and a wispy puff of smoke rose from the chimney.

"Where in the name of God have you been?" his father yelled the instant Jamie walked in. "Why'd you take off like that? What's wrong with you, lad? You were rude to the good doctor."

Jamie smelled liquor on his father's breath. He tried to hold on to his feeling of calm, but the alcohol and the shouted words "the good doctor" shattered it.

"How can you say that? 'The good doctor!'" he yelled back. "Look what he did to Ma!"

"Hush your mouth! You dinna know what you're talkin' about!" His father took a step toward him, fists clenched.

The sight of those fists ready to strike out scared Jamie. Had he finally gone too far? His father had never hit him. It simply wasn't in him to be violent. This wasn't his fault. It was the damn liquor talking. Summoning whatever courage he had, he lashed out. "So now, are you gonna hit me? Is this what the drink's done, Da?"

His father's head whipped back as if he had taken an unexpected punch. He dropped his fists, grabbed a chair, and collapsed into it like a limp, rag doll. When a deep sigh escaped his lips, it was as if all the air in him leaked out, until all that remained was a deflated and defeated man.

To his horror, Jamie watched tears form in his father's eyes. Uncertain what to do, he stood immobilized. Da wasn't a man to cry. Except for that day. The day his ma died. For perhaps the first time since, Jamie truly understood his father's loss had been every bit as great as his. He'd been so lost in his own grief he'd been blind to his da's. Robbie had Melinda and a new baby coming. He and Da were left here with nothing but each other.

His da also seemed immobilized by uncertainty, not even bothering to brush away his tears, which left streaks on his stubbly cheeks. Jamie's alarm at his father's condition forced him to speak first. "I'll put the kettle on." His father simply nodded.

Chapter Thirteen

Fishing for Pies

Saturday morning, Jamie awoke early, prepared to meet Carr and put into action the plan to help themselves to some of Mrs. Robertson's pies. He'd anticipated the adventure all week, working himself into a state of high excitement. He was tired of always being with his da, who'd become a sad old man, and even Robbie, who might as well be an old man, the way he acted with Melinda these days. It would be a welcome change hanging around with someone different, and as strange as Carr might be, at least the fellow knew how to laugh.

In moments of brutal honesty, however, he had to admit to moments of being torn. On the one hand, part of him yearned for some real fun, as well as some of those mouth-watering pies like his mother used to make. On the other hand, it was being reminded of his mother that made him hesitate. He knew how disappointed in him she would have been, but he'd managed to push all that aside and gone to bed determined to follow through.

However, as he carried out his morning chores and ate a quick and mostly silent breakfast with his father, these conflicting thoughts rose again. Finally, after an agony of indecision, at the very last minute, he just plain got cold feet. He couldn't go through with the plan.

*****

Although it was still early April the ice was gone in some areas, so instead of meeting Carr, Jamie packed a simple lunch, grabbed his fishing pole, and set out for his favourite spot beside a quiet little pool of open water. It might be too early in the season for speckled trout to bite, but he wanted to try, If he didn't catch anything, he'd be content being outside on such a fine day doing something he enjoyed. If he was lucky, fresh fish would be a treat. No matter how optimistic he tried to be about the situation, however, there was one thing he had to admit: no fish could ever compare to a pie. But at least if he brought a fish home, he'd have come by it honestly.

At the water's edge, he bent down and scooped up a handful of water so frigid, it caused his body to shiver as he swallowed. Overnight rain had resulted in muddy banks, and after half an hour slip-sliding in the muck, trying to catch a few worms for bait, he had enough and put the first one on his line. By mid-morning, his efforts were rewarded; two good-sized trout hung from a line in a pine tree, out of reach of most animals who might be attracted by their scent. His da would be pleased with his catch.

Since he'd barely eaten any breakfast, he decided to unpack his lunch early. Sitting on the sloped bank under the same pine, he sat back to enjoy the welcome sunshine. Although the pond was close to the edge of the village, a peaceful silence enveloped him. He was alone in this perfect spot. Or so he thought.

"What the hell are ya doin' here, MacGregor?

The blacksmith's son's sudden appearance behind him startled Jamie so much he dropped his piece of bread. Carr laughed, as Jamie brushed bits of dirt off it.

"What d'you want?" Jamie asked, refusing to turn around.

"Wha' do I want? You were s'posed to meet me this mornin'. Did ya forget the plan?"

Jamie remained silent, munching on his bread, although his appetite had disappeared.

Behind him, he heard a noisy sniff. "I c'n almost smell ol' lady Robertson's pies all the way over here. We gotta move fast…now! I want at least one o' those pies. Two each, if we can do it."

"Changed my mind." Jamie tried for non-chalance.

"Waddya mean, changed your mind? We agreed. Man, those pies'd taste a helluva lot better'n that dry bread you're chewin' on."

Jamie had had enough. Anger rose like bile in his throat and his words tumbled out before he had time to think. "I said I changed my mind. What's the matter, Carr? Can't your own mother bake pies? Or is she a lazy, good-for-nothing slob like you?"

"You shut your damned mouth, MacGregor! I'll kill you." Carr's fist shot out fast, too fast. He lost his footing on the riverbank and skidded, arms flailing, as he fought to maintain his balance.

"You're nuts, Carr! I told you I'm not stealin' anything. Get lost!" Jamie's words sounded braver than he felt, for Carr's face was distorted with a frightening expression.

Without warning, that fearful expression transformed into a grin, but it wasn't a pleasant sight. His angry face reddened until it almost matched his shirt. A shirt, Jamie noted, that looked oddly like the one Carr had urged him to steal from the store not long ago. Had he taken it himself at some point? If he did, he's got a lot o' nerve walking around in it, Jamie thought. Either that, or he's just plain stupid. Andrew Whylie is sure to know if one's missing. He'd spot it in a minute.

Like lightening, Carr's sick, angry grin disappeared, replaced in a flash by a knowing smirk. "I get it, you got cold feet."

"I did not!..."

"Yeah, ya did. But it's all right. No problem." Carr waved off Jamie's protest. "Just means all the more pie for me. I guess I got ya wrong. Thought you wanted a few laughs, a bit of fun."

"There's fun, and there's stealin'," Jamie said.

"Fine. If that's the way you want it..." Carr turned and slipped back through the trees, presumably heading for Mrs. Robertson's.

Jamie's mind rattled back and forth with conflicting emotions. Would Carr actually go through with it, or was it all a bluff? He'd probably stolen that red shirt he was wearing, so why would he hesitate to take some pies?

His head throbbed. He couldn't imagine stealing Mrs. Robertson's pies or anything else, but mesmerized by this strange individual, he felt compelled to follow and see what happened. Maybe, with luck, he could put a stop to it.

Chapter Fourteen

Too Close for Comfort

Following the same path through the trees, Jamie came out on the muddy road and spied Carr moving in a quick, determined fashion, covering more ground than he'd expected. Jamie let out a deafening whistle to catch his attention. Somewhere nearby a hound dog set up a mournful howling. At any other time, it might have been comical, but not today.

Carr stopped and looked back, a satisfied smile spreading across his cocky face. "Changed your mind after all? That's great. We'll have some real fun."

"Just thought I'd go along to watch. I don't want any pie."

"You'll change your mind." Carr appeared definite. "I know," he nodded, as if for emphasis."

Jamie thought it better not to reply.

"No time to waste. Let's go! You head on over to the Robertson place. I'll follow. I don't want anyone seein' us together, got it?"

"Why should I go first? You're the one wants the pies."

Carr shook his head. "Ya sure got a lot t' learn. Nobody'd suspect you o' bein' up to anythin', Jamie boy. That's why." He laughed. "Remember that carrot up your…"

"Shut up!" Jamie shot back, but he followed his instructions.

Not wanting to be seen on the road heading to Mrs. Robertson's, Jamie remained alert as he crossed through fields and bush behind the stores and houses. He managed to make his way without encountering anyone and prayed no one was watching, but he couldn't be certain.

The tantalizing aroma of apples and cinnamon grew stronger as he approached. His favourite kind of pie. Despite his best resolve, his mouth watered, and sharp hunger pangs cramped his stomach. When at last he spied the pies on the windowsill, he tried not to think about what he was about to do. He'd made a decision and simply had to get it over with.

Carefully scouting the yard and woods behind him, he spotted a red shirt behind a tree and thought what an enormous chance the jerk was taking by wearing something to easy to spot, and something probably stolen at that! To his relief, no one else seemed to be around.

Carr caught his eye and, pointing to the house, nodded to him to go first. "Why me?" Jamie wanted to argue, but Carr had dipped out of sight again.

He closed his eyes for a second, then looked at the pies again, and swore under his breath. "It's now or never," he said to himself, working up his courage. "Just do it!"

It wasn't as if he was stealing money, he reasoned. Mrs. Robertson could always bake more pies. These attempts to justify his actions fell flat. He knew what he was about to do was wrong. Wiping sweat out of his eyes again, he tiptoed forward in slow motion. Why the hell am I tip-toeing? He almost laughed at the absurdity. It'd be better to be fast. Get in and out as fast as he could.

Jamie took off at a run and made it to the window. As he grasped a warm pie plate, something stopped him. Was it his conscience kicking in at last, or simply fear of getting caught? Whatever it was, he knew he couldn't do this. But Carr was watching. He had to think of something fast. His mind raced with possibilities.

It seemed like forever but was only a matter of a split second before he decided. Near his right foot lay an empty metal bucket. In one swift move, Jamie turned and kicked it against the house, trying to make it appear as if he'd accidentally tripped over it, making a great show of stumbling around.

With a clang, the bucket hit the wall, bounced off and rattled even more loudly against a small boulder. At the same time, the metal pie plate he'd let go of, slid off the window sill and hit the ground hard. It was enough to start a dog yapping in the house. Thankfully, it sounded like a small one. He sure didn't fancy being chased and attached by some huge beast.

Above all the racket, and the deafening sound of his own racing heart as he made his escape, he could hear a voice somewhere behind him. "Princess!" a woman called, "What on earth are you carrying on about, girl?" The voice came closer to the window. "What is it, girl?"

Jamie dove into some tall underbrush and lay flat on the ground. He sneaked a look back at the very moment Mrs.

Robertson's grey head appeared at the window. "Oh, dear!" she lamented. "I've lost a pie! Now, how did that happen?"

From the corner of his eye, Jamie saw a red flash as Carr took off from his hiding spot, that shirt as visible as a target. At the same moment, Mrs. Robertson opened her window further and leaned out. She must have put two and two together. "Stop!" she cried out. "Stop, I say! I know who you are. Just wait till your father hears."

When she disappeared from the window, presumably heading for her door to come outside, Jamie saw his chance for a get-away and sprinted harder than he ever had in his life. Behind one of the houses, he spied a shed with its door ajar and raced inside, where he slipped and skidded on the muddy, dirt floor. A dreadful, reeking stink hit him. He knew for sure it wasn't skunk, but it was foul. Maybe there was a dead animal decaying in sone of the dark corners. The stench sickened him, but he didn't dare step back outside. Even though Mrs. Robertson hadn't seen him, it would be smart to lay low for a while.

*****

An hour or so later, as he skirted the edge of town, Jamie wasn't at all surprised to find Carr standing in his way. Before the brute could speak, Jamie blurted out, "I didn't see the stupid bucket, and then the damn dog started up."

"You really messed up, you frickin' idiot! Ol' lady Robertson marched right over and told my father I tried to steal her pies."

"Look, I'm sorry. I didn't mean to..." Jamie saw the punch coming and ducked.

"Get back here!" a deep voice thundered. "What'd I tell ya? You don't go anywhere until I say so, ya good-for-nothing! Ya got work to do."

Jamie was shocked at how frightening anger in Mr. Carr's deep scarlet face. He wouldn't want to be the one facing that man's wrath. When he glanced at young Carr, he observed the colour drain from his face and his entire body twitch. Then, from somewhere deep within, the fellow summoned an air of defiance, lifted his chin and sauntered back towards the blacksmith's shop.

As he passed his father, the man moved faster than a whip and smacked him across the face. Still, his son kept his head up and continued walking until he disappeared from sight. When the blacksmith turned his furious gaze back in his direction, Jamie took off and didn't stop running until he was almost home.

Pulling up at the side of the road, he heaved deep breaths, trying to slow his heartbeat and gather himself together before he saw his own father. The last thing he needed now was further questioning about anything. Without warning, a wave of nausea hit him and his stomach twisted and wretched. He thought he would vomit, but as he hadn't eaten for hours, there was nothing on his stomach.

In fact, remembering that bit of bread he'd been chewing on hours ago, when Carr interrupted his fishing, reminded him that he'd left behind his pole, as well as the two fish he'd caught. Slapping himself up the side of the head, he swore. "Friggin' idiot!" He could go back for his pole tomorrow, but no doubt some bear had already enjoyed the fish.

Slumping against a tree, he tried to gather his wits about him. He'd thought he was being clever kicking that bucket over, but all he'd done was make things worse. Carr would surely want revenge. It would be wise to stay out of his way until he'd had a chance to cool down, if he ever did.

Trying to find a bright spot in all this mess, he thought that at least he could truthfully claim he was not a thief, although he'd come close, too damn close for comfort. The fact that he'd managed to avoid stealing lifted his spirits momentarily. However, he knew this good feeling was probably temporary. Carr seemed like the kind who wouldn't give up trying to involve him in what he called "fun": the kind of fun that could get a person in serious trouble. Like what happened today. He thought again of the blacksmith's furious fist striking out at his son and young Carr's defiant head held high, as he walked away.

For Jamie, reflecting on the day's disaster, the most confusing realization was that part of him still found the idea of hanging around this strange newcomer intriguing. He'd never met anyone like him before.

Despite everything, Jamie knew it wouldn't take much persuading to get him caught up in another of Carr's risky adventures. Acknowledging this shook him to his core. He wasn't just confused; he was certain he was losing his mind. If only there was someone, anyone, he could talk to. Once upon a time, he'd have gone to Robbie, or maybe even his ma. Now, there was no one.

Chapter Fifteen

A Fine Looking Girl

Jamie bounced on the seat of the old wagon as it creaked along the rough road. With every spring thaw, frost erupted from the frozen ground, causing at best an uneven surface, and at its worst, a dangerous one. A wheel could break loose, a wagon could overturn, even more devastating, a horse might slip and break a leg.

His father held the reins, concentrating so intently on guiding their mare, Annie, that he didn't speak. Jamie was just as pleased. He felt bad about the recent shouting match between the two of them, but part of him was glad he'd confronted his da. One day his father would have to face the reality of what had happened. Maybe he would even come round to Jamie's side about the doctor – the doctor! Now Jamie couldn't stop thinking about him and it made his head just ache.

He became alert as they entered the village. Not wanting to see or talk to anyone, especially the blacksmith's son, he cast an uneasy glance around the places where the wretch usually lurked and was relieved to see no sign of him. Jamie had tried to stay home, but his father had insisted he needed him. As they pulled up in front of the general store, he decided to make an attempt at being conciliatory, "I'll hitch her up, Da. You go in ahead." He received a curt grunt in reply.

He watched his father shuffle up the three steps to the door like an old man. He wasn't all that old, but he looked ancient since he'd started drinking and not caring how he looked.

In the store, his da would likely meet a neighbour or two, and he'd want to catch up with whatever news there was. Farmers could talk endlessly about the weather, and which crops were doing well, and which ones were a disappointment.

Jamie didn't want to hang around town long, but maybe it would be good if his father enjoyed himself for a while. Maybe things would look up at home...unless a farmer started in on local politics or on how the village was growing too fast, which might drag his da even deeper into depression. Or worse, what if someone began to gossip about the wedding or had beard about the pie incident. So many things to worry about- could his life be more complicated? Anyway, he decided he best go inside and check on the situation.

Jumping down from the wagon, he hitched it to a post. Still vigilant, he looked around once again for signs he was being watched. Nothing. Still, he felt nervous and found himself turning to their horse to ease the tension.

Stroking Annie's nose, soothing her, telling her she was a good old girl and how fine she looked, somehow helped him to feel a little better himself. The animal's immense, dark eyes seemed to look into the depths of his and understand. She shook her mane and pawed the ground, as if pleased with the compliment.

"Yes, you sure are a fine-looking girl," Jamie repeated with one last pat on her nose. "Fine looking." Just then, he looked up to see a girl his age come to a halt in front of him. He hadn't noticed her coming out of the store. Her mass of shiny, brown curls bounced as she tilted her head, and her hazel eyes were set off by the dark green of her simple dress. He was sure he'd never seen her before. He would have remembered those eyes that were now taking him in. He watched her mouth form a bemused smile, and a terrible thought struck him. Does she think I was talking to her? He recalled his words to Annie. "You sure are a fine-looking girl."

Despite his embarrassment, he ventured a discreet look from under his cap. She was still watching him. But this time, he noted with some satisfaction, it was her turn to blush, and with a toss of those curls, she turned and headed across the road. As he turned to enter the store, he couldn't resist a backward glance, but she was nowhere in sight. Who is she? he wondered. Why haven't I seen her around before?

Inside, he discovered that, despite all his worries about gossip and talk of failed crops, his father was the sole customer. This pleased him as it meant they could leave as soon as they had their supplies. Jamie moved about, pretending to examine the shelves, taking in everything, and yet he absorbed nothing. He was thinking about the girl. He could still see the smile on her face and felt himself blushing again. What a stupid clod I am! Talking like that to a horse. Whoever she is, she'll go tell her friends, and they'll all have a good laugh. Since he didn't recognize her, he wondered if maybe she wasn't from the area. With luck, he might not ever see her again, and that might be just as well. He'd be too embarrassed to face her. But still he kept thinking about her.

*****

Andrew Whylie, hauling a fifty-pound sack of flour from the storeroom, paused when he noticed Jamie's father examining an axe, hefting it in his hand to test its weight.

"Are you in need of an axe, Mr. MacGregor? I could give you a little off the price."

"No, thanks, Andrew. Just admirin' it. What I do need is some oats. And a couple o' pounds of coffee, too, I guess."

Breaking through his thoughts, Jamie noticed Andrew struggling with the heavy sack, and couldn't help being sorry for him. He knew how awful he'd feel if an accident put him in that shape.

"Here, can I take that for you? " He stepped forward to relieve Andrew of his load, then immediately wondered if he'd done the right thing. Would Andrew be insulted?

"Thanks. Appreciate it." To Jamie's relief, Andrew was pleased by his offer. Hands on hips, the storekeeper leaned back as if to ease his aching back. "M-m-m, that helps."

Mr. MacGregor showed concern. "Is it getting any better at all?"

"Actually, it is, thanks. Dr. Paul has been trying some new treatments on me, and they seem to be helping."

"He's a good man."

"He sure is. I'm lucky he's right here, in the village. We all are."

"Aye, that we are."

At this, Jamie felt the familiar flash of anger. He wanted to yell but instead dropped the heavy sack where it belonged and hurried out the door, thinking that surely it couldn't get worse than this.

Outside, he closed his eyes, trying to control his anger. When will it ever end? he wondered. When he opened his eyes, his father came to stand beside him. "What're you doin' standin' out here? There's supplies need to be loaded up."

Heading back inside, Jamie heard a horse snorting as a buggy approached. From the corner of his eye, he caught a glimpse of colour, a familiar dark green he'd seen not twenty minutes earlier. That girl! Quick! How could he hide?

Before he could slip inside and out of sight, his father called out, "Mornin', Doctor."

"Morning, Ian. Jamie."

Gripped by agony, Jamie knew he had no choice but to reply. With great reluctance, he turned around. There sat the girl beside Dr. Paul in his buggy. Why? In his confusion, he barely managed to mutter, "Mornin'".

Dr. Paul nodded in reply, but the pretty girl in the green dress favoured him with a smile full of sunshine.

"Now there's a bonnie lass," his father commented.

Jamie tried for a nonchalant manner. "I guess so. Who is she?" he asked, despite a sinking feeling he already knew the answer.

"Why, that's the doctor's step-daugh

Chapter Sixteen

Sunday Dinner

Sundays were the hardest. Jamie missed his ma more on that day than any other. She had always enjoyed cooking a big meal for her family, trying to make the day special, especially after Robbie and Melinda were married.

His mother had been very fond of her daughter-in-law, and his da still was. Melinda seemed to feel the same way about them, and, at the start, she was fine with him, too. She did tend to treat him as Robbie's little brother, which was annoying, because she wasn't that much older than he was, but still, she was all right. What had brought about such a change in her? As always, Jamie wondered what he'd done wrong.

After the morning chores were finished, a long afternoon and evening stretched ahead, with his father lost in his own thoughts. Jamie found the cabin's resulting silence claustrophobic, so when his ears picked up the faint sound of a wagon bumping over the rough terrain, he leaped to his feet and rushed to the window to investigate.

"What's up, lad?" His father seemed confused, as if waking from a dream state.

"Someone's comin'. It sounds like…it is! It's Robbie!"

"Robbie? Is he alone?"

With far less enthusiasm, Jamie reported, "No. Melinda's with him."

"Somethin' must be wrong," his da exclaimed, rousing himself to get up and open the door.

"Is everythin' all right?" he asked, relieving Melinda of the basket she carried.

"Everything's fine," Robbie reassured him. "Thought you might like some company, that's all, so we decided to come for dinner."

"Well, thank the good Lord everythin's all right," Da replied, with a broad smile of relief.

Jamie thought how long it had been since he'd seen his father smile about anything and was glad this unexpected visit had brought one about.

"But I don't know what we've got to offer..." his father started to fuss, before Melinda pointed to a bundle Robbie was carrying, "We brought a chicken and some fixin's. There's plenty for all of us."

"What a good lass you are," Mr.MacGregor enthused, "Let's get it on the stove."

Melinda, looking much healthier than the last time Jamie had seen her, busied herself with the meal, Robbie and his da caught up on news of their neighbours. Jamie, pleased to see his brother and the change in their father's mood, hoped this was a sign things of things looking up. Maybe they could really be a family again, even though it would never be the same without his ma, maybe it could be something new.

*****

Hours later, Jamie lay in bed wondering how things had gone so wrong. He'd only been trying to help. Melinda had become somewhat frazzled getting dinner together. Things weren't as clean and orderly as when his ma was in charge of cooking. There'd been trouble with the stove; the fire hadn't caught well, and the chicken took forever to cook.

By the time everything else was ready, and it was time to make the gravy, Melinda's red face and slumped back indicated how tired she was. Wanting to help, Jamie said, " Here, I'll lift the chicken out for you."

"No, no. I can do it," Melinda protested, opening the oven door and grabbing a towel for lifting the hot pan.

"It's all right. I can do it," Jamie insisted and reached for the towel. But Melinda was not to be deterred, and as she grabbed the pan, she and Jamie collided.

Amid shrieks and shouts, the pan hit the floor. Hot grease sizzled and oozed in a widening circle. The chicken slid under the stove. Da lunged for the bird, and swearing that his fingers were burned, flung it on top of the table. Robbie caught Melinda, as she lost her balance, sliding in the hot grease. Da, too, slipped, landing on his rear end, his pants soaking up hot, greasy stains.

"Ow-w-w!" he yelled. "My backside's burnt." Jamie helped him to his feet, then stood immobilized by fear and the enormity of the mess he'd caused. Three pairs of eyes stared at him. He realized he was trembling.

"I'm sorry!" he whispered.

Melinda moaned, "Look at the grease all over my best dress! And my shoes! It'll never come out." She began to cry. "And my dinner. Everything's ruined."

"It'll be fine," Robbie attempted to console her. "The important thing is you're all right. At least you didn't fall." Shaking his head, he glared at Jamie. "What were you thinking? If she'd gone down, she could have lost the baby, for God's sake!"

'Lost the baby'. The hurled accusation stunned Jamie into silence. He didn't know what to do or say.

Melinda remained inconsolable, sobbing in deep, noisy gasps. Alarmed, her father-in-law rushed to soothe her. "It's no so bad, lass. At least the dog's outside, or he'd have taken off with that chicken in a heartbeat!"

When the smile he'd hoped for didn't appear, he said, "Come now, we can still enjoy it. We don't need gravy. Robbie and I'll dish up the potatoes and carrots. You just sit, lass, and dinna worry. We'll be fine."

When he looked at Jamie, the upbeat manner he'd attempted for Melinda's sake, disappeared. His shoulders slumped, and frustration showed in his eyes. "Get the mop, boy," he said in a voice so low Jamie strained to hear. "And get this mess off the floor."

*****

Eventually, the four MacGregors had sat down to a tense Sunday dinner together, with Melinda remaining upset, Da having little to say, Robbie straining to stay calm, and himself wishing all the while he was anywhere else but at that table.

Not surprisingly, Melinda and Robbie departed early. After the door closed behind them, Jamie and his father each went to their own bed in a suffocating and painful silence.

And now, here he lay in the absolute darkness of his room, depressed, and going over and over the day's unhappy events in his mind. As dawn broke, Jamie drifted off into a trouble sleep, wondering if this was how his life was going to be from now on, one disaster after another.

Chapter Seventeen

The Watcher

Like a prickly burr stuck inside his trousers, the memory of that disastrous Sunday dinner tormented Jamie for some time. He'd fall into a dark mood, wondering if his family would ever be a real family again. He hadn't thought he'd miss some of the little things his mother cared about, like celebrating birthdays and Sunday dinners. Now he realized they weren't little things at all; they were important, more important than he could have ever known when he was younger. Back then, he often complained about what he thought was just a lot of fuss.

In one of these moods, as he tramped through the fresh-smelling woods, unaware of the delightful day or the profusion of early wildflowers at his feet, he stumbled upon a scene guaranteed to sink him even deeper into self-pity. On the road skirting the woods, the entire Paul family laughed and chatted as they walked together, probably on their way home from some friend's house. Watching the little girls skipping ahead and giggling as they sang a nursery rhyme, while the others followed in high spirits, reminded him of a watching a small parade. Not that he'd ever seen a parade, but he imagined that's what one would look like.

"What have they got to be so happy about?" he grumbled to himself. Still, he was sufficiently intrigued by the group to follow them, sticking to the woods and keeping out of sight.

He recognized the pretty girl, walking with her brother, Caleb, at the rear of the group. They kept up a lively conversation, which he strained to overhear, but the distance was too great and he had to be careful. Once, Caleb stopped and turned around as if he'd heard something, causing Jamie to duck behind a tree.

He followed the happy parade all the way to town, attracted by their sense of ease with each other. They were simply enjoying the beautiful day and just being together. When a sharp stabbing feeling caught him in the chest, it only took a moment for him to recognized it for what it was: jealousy. He wanted what this family had for himself and his own family.

What's left of it, he thought. What would it take to change things for the MacGregors? He couldn't imagine.

Dejected, he observed the family enter their home. Only when the door closed behind them, did he realize someone else was also watching.

*****

"Just out for a walk, were ya'?

Jamie swung around, his furious fists raised.

The familiar smirk made it clear that while he'd been watching the doctor's family, he'd been under observation himself.

"None o' your damn business." He took a menacing step forward, which to his amazement, caused Carr to take a half-step back.

"Now, now. No need to get all worked up. We're pals, aren't we?

Jamie said nothing.

"Besides, you and me got a lot in common. I know exactly what you were thinkin'. What have they got to be so happy about? Right? How come everythin' goes their way, but not for you an' me?"

It shocked Jamie to hear his own thoughts echoed. It never occurred to him that anyone else might feel like he did. He didn't respond, afraid to give Carr the satisfaction of knowing he was right.

Carr sauntered off, once again leaving Jamie stunned and confused. But the so-and-so wasn't finished. He turned and called back, "Don't know about you, but me, I got big plans. One o' these days, I'm gonna have all that, too. Big house. Nice clothes. Just you wait. " Then, he threw his head back and let out a shrill, maniacal cackle before taking off at a run.

Before Jamie could process what had been said, a stranger raced past him and up to the doctor's house, where he banged on the door. While waiting for an answer, he jumped from foot to foot with impatience, and when the door opened, his wild gesticulations indicated an urgency.

Within minutes, the doctor emerged, medical bag in hand, and moments later led Armon out of a shed and hitched him to his buggy. As they set off, Jamie could see that the frantic stranger seated on the front bench beside Dr. Paul was a young man not much older than himself. Despite his own black mood, further aggravated by Carr's unexpected appearance, a stirring of compassion arose. At the same time, he fumed watching the buggy bounce and creak down the road. "Who's he going off to let die now?" he muttered.

Unable to stop himself, he followed the buggy at a distance, staying out of sight as best he could. When it slowed and turned up a narrow, slightly-overgrown lane, Jamie knew he should let it go and head home. This obsession with Dr. Paul was crazy; he realized that. However, some force he couldn't resist impelled him up the lane, which soon widened to reveal a newly-built cabin.

The middle-aged man who stepped out to greet the doctor looked strangely familiar. Then it struck him: this man's deeply-lined face bore the same desperately worried expression his own father's had when his ma was sick. And here was Dr. Paul come to "help" the patient again! At this painful reminder, his head began to spin, and an extreme dizziness overtook him. Everything was suddenly all too much. His heart and mind raced, knowing he had to get out of there, yet his feet refused to move. To his horror, tears stung his eyes. In a fog of emotions, he looked around, wondering what to do next.

His familiar rage surged, along with a desire to lash out, to inflict harm. Someone had to put an end to all the damage this so-called doctor was doing. But he couldn't attack the man. He'd get caught, for sure. Whatever he decided to do, it mustn't point back to him. Jamming his hands in his pockets, the fingers of one hand touched cold metal. His pocketknife. Yes!

Approaching Armon with stealth, he kept his eyes on the cabin to make sure no one was watching. If the door opened, he'd have to dive into the bushes. A tightness in his throat left him breathless, and sweat now mingled with the dried tears on his face. Armon sensed his presence and snickered.

"Sh-h-h! Good boy," Jamie whispered, patting the animal's flanks. When he was certain it wasn't going to panic and sound an alarm, he flicked open his knife's sharp blade, and with one swift movement, slit the harness under its belly. Armon backed up and one powerful hoof lashed out, but Jamie dodged the blow and took off down the lane, not slowing until he was some distance along the main road. There he stopped to rest and take stock of what he'd done.

With luck, when Dr. Paul picked up the reins and urged Armon forward, the harness would fall apart. He'd probably have to unhitch his horse and walk him home. It was unlikely he'd try riding him without a saddle. Maybe he'd even have to leave his buggy behind. Well, that would put an end to the doctor's "rounds" for a while. Jamie didn't intend to stick around and find out, but for the first time in that entire dark day, he noticed the sun was shining, lifted his face to its warmth, and smiled.

Chapter Eighteen

The MacGregor Crest

Joseph Paul finished his tea, having refused Ian MacGregor's offer of "just a wee dram" of whisky several times. On another occasion, he'd have enjoyed it, but he had one more call to make and needed to remain alert. Whiskey tended to make him sleepy, particularly in the afternoon. Besides, he had a suspicion his host had already taken a few "drams" and wondered if this might be becoming a problem. He'd always thought of MacGregor as a steady man, not given to overindulging in any way. However, losing a loved one was a severe blow and not everyone coped well. The man had to be lonely, even with Jamie here. Well, he could sympathize. The loss of his own first wife had left him aching with loneliness, and yet he'd still had his darling Heather.

He stood up, reaching for his bag. "Well, I thank you for the tea, Ian. It's warmed me up nicely, and I should be going. Tell Jamie I'm sorry I missed him."

"I'll do that. God only knows where he's off to today. But stop by anytime, Doctor. You'll always find a welcome."

Pushing himself out of his chair, Ian MacGregor stretched his back. "Here, don't forget your hat!" He nodded to indicate a peg by the door where the hat perched.

As the doctor retrieved it, he noticed a small, carved wooden shield hung above the peg. He'd seen it before but not paid close attention. Now, he couldn't take his eyes off it.

"What is it?"

"Oh, nothing, really." Now that he'd been caught staring, he became flustered and felt foolish for what seemed like subterfuge, but he had to know the meaning of the carving on the shield. "I noticed this shield. I mean, I've seen it before, when I made my calls on Sarah, but I didn't pay much attention. Is it a family crest or something?"

"Of a kind. My father made it in the old country. It's one of the few things we brought wi' us. A wee reminder of home."

"I see." Dr. Paul paused before asking what was, to him, the most important question, "And what are those symbols?"

"They're supposed to be a lion's head with a crown. I guess they don't look much like it, if you didn't know. Da wasna much of a carver. He claimed they were from the

MacGregor coat of arms, meaning MacGregors are from royalty. Though how he'd know I'm not sure. We were too poor to have a coat of arms like the clan chiefs."

*****

The doctor clicked his tongue, signaling Armon to move along. With a heavy heart he thought about the symbols on the MacGregors' shield. He believed he'd seen them somewhere else: on the sling-shot Caleb showed him. And he couldn't deny the initials carved on it likely stood for Jamie MacGregor. If Caleb's theory was correct, the person who lost the slingshot is the one who broke the window, and the evidence pointed to the boy. He shook his head in confusion, his mind overflowing with questions. What could possibly have driven Jamie MacGregor to such a senseless act? Why would he want to interrupt a wedding in such a frightening manner? However, about one thing the doctor was certain. He and young MacGregor were going to have a talk.

*****

With a nod of his head, his step-father indicated to Caleb that he wished to see him in the office down the hall. After they'd entered, he closed the door and locked it for privacy.

"Have a seat," he said, pointing to a chair. Taking his own seat behind his desk, he leaned back, and released a long sigh.

To Caleb, it was obvious his step-father had something on his mind, so he waited for him to speak. When he did, a surprising note of sadness tinged his words. "I believe I know who the slingshot belongs to."

A current of excitement charged through Caleb. He jumped up from his seat and demanded, "Who?" He was still furious and needed to know why that rock had been tossed through the window on his mother's wedding day.

Dr. Paul hesitated. Caleb sensed a reluctance to speak the name aloud. But why? Unable to bear the suspense, he demanded once more, "Who is it?"

"I believe it's Jamie MacGregor." This was uttered more with regret than any pleasure or excitement in solving the mystery. Caleb couldn't understand this reaction.

"MacGregor? I've seen him around." Caleb searched his mind for some memory, some reason why the kid might be the one. "But why would he want to do somethin' like this? Is he crazy?" he demanded. "Or d'you think it was just a stupid prank?" he asked, more hopefully. When his step-father shook his head in confusion, Caleb continued probing. " If it wasn't a prank, does that mean he might have something against you? Some kind of grudge?

"I don't know! That's the problem. I used to see him when I made calls on his poor mother. He was a very quiet lad, but I never thought he was a trouble-maker. Or even a prankster, for that matter." Rubbing his chin in puzzlement, Joseph Paul stared at his desk top as if the answer lay there.

"Naturally, the boy was distraught when his mother died, but why would that lead to such a destructive act? I believe there was intense anger behind throwing that rock." He looked up at Caleb. "But at whom could he be so angry? It couldn't be your mother!"

"And why choose to act out during the wedding? Why not some other time?"

"I don't know!" Now the doctor, too, was on his feet, pacing behind his desk. "That's what's so darned frustrating."

Caleb hesitated before putting his thoughts into words. He didn't want to hurt his step-father. But it had to be said, because maybe whatever was going on wasn't going to stop with that rock. Maybe there was more to come. "I don't like to say this, but…if he wasn't acting out against Ma, then it must have been aimed at you. If it was anyone else, he could have picked a different time."

Dr. Paul dropped back into his chair and closed his eyes. "I have to admit I've been wondering the same thing," he said in a weary tone. "As soon as he saw me last week, he took off like a jack-rabbit into the bush and didn't come back all the time I was there. He was avoiding me. His father even apologized for the boy's rudeness."

"You said his ma died. D'ya think that has somethin' to do with this?"

"I considered that, too. Sarah MacGregor died of pneumonia, and her death was a tragic loss. But it was also, unfortunately, a normal progression of the illness."

Caleb was fuming. How could his step-father remain so calm? It was his wedding that had been interrupted. "People die all the time. Their families don't go insane like that. It's no excuse."

"Take it easy. If there's one thing I've learned, it's that people handle grief differently." Dr. Paul was thoughtful, as if trying to recall more details.

"There was nothing unusual about Sarah MacGregor's passing. But I need to talk to the young man. If it was him, and I'm the one he's upset with, this needs straightening out."

Caleb's patience was running low. "What good will talking do? He'll only deny it."

His step-father raised his voice in rebuke. "And what would you suggest? Remember, when it comes right down to it, we have no actual proof it was him. The sling-shot means nothing, even if it does have his initials. There were no witnesses."

"Well, maybe we haven't look hard enough," Caleb said as he walked out. "Maybe somebody did see something. I'm going to find out."

Chapter Nineteen

Come into My Office

Jamie was near the rear of the store, when the tinkle of the bell above the door broke into his thoughts. He and his father had been in town less than an hour, but still, he'd been on the lookout, expecting to see young Carr at any moment. His body tensed as he waited for the usual sneering comment, but it was a different voice that spoke.

"Good morning, Ian."

Jamie turned as his father replied, "'Mornin', Doc."

He watched Andrew nod in greeting. "Anything I can help you with, Dr. Paul?"

"Thanks, Andrew, but I've found what I'm looking for."

What was that supposed to mean? The man hadn't even looked around the store yet. Intent on avoiding him, Jamie moved further back. However, he was curious enough to want to hear whatever else might be said, so he tried staying within listening distance.

"I was actually looking for you, Ian," he heard the doctor say. "Would you mind coming over to my office for a few minutes when you're finished here? I'd like to discuss something with you."

Raising his voice slightly, he added, "You, too, Jamie. If you don't mind."

Caught! Jamie cursed himself under his breath. "Stupid! Should've moved further back. Never mind trying to hear what he had to say. Now, I have to answer the man.

"What d'you want me for?" he blurted out.

"Don't be rude, son! If the doctor needs to talk to both of us, you'll come."

His father turned to Dr. Paul. "I don't know what the boy's thinkin'. We'll be there shortly." His voice became anxious. "Is everythin' all right? What's this about?"

"I'd rather not discuss anything here. I'll see you shortly." The doctor smiled, nodded to all three, and walked back out of the store.

Jamie was furious. Now, he had to go and talk to the man. In his office. He couldn't escape it. What the heck did he want, anyway? Did he know? He couldn't! There was no way. As hard as he tried to convince himself, deep down, he wasn't so sure. Had someone seen him after all? Was it Caleb? No, he'd have said something sooner. Who then?

"Let's get a move on," his father was saying.

Jamie's head snapped up. "What?' he asked.

Frustration showed on his father's weary face. And his eyes held the usual disappointment. "Where's your head these days?" he sighed. "I said, 'Let's get a move on. Dr. Paul's waitin'"

As he followed in his father's muddy tracks across the rutted road, an unexpected touch of early spring sunshine warmed Jamie's face. Looking up, he noted the day's earlier dark clouds had vanished. Maybe this was a sign. Maybe he was getting all worked up over nothing. Maybe this wasn't about the wedding after all, but something completely different. Sure, that's what it was. He clutched this thought to his pounding heart, as if it were a lifeline.

*****

Ian MacGregor stood, hat in hand, running calloused fingers through his tangled hair, trying to improve his appearance, before Heather Paul answered his knock and greeted them.

"Good morning, Mr. MacGregor. My father's waiting for you in his office. And how are you, Jamie? I've missed you in school these past few months. I hope you're planning to come back."

For the second time in recent days, Jamie blushed before a pretty girl. Shyness wasn't his only problem; he also didn't know what to say. He'd missed so much school, he didn't see the point in going back. "Thank you, Miss," he mumbled.

"He can go back if he wants to." His father's words flabbergasted him. "It's what his mother wanted. Sarah had more learnin' than any of us MacGregors. She wanted that for her boys, too." Da stopped, as if embarrassed to have said so much.

The mention of his mother reminded Jamie again of where he was standing at the moment, in whose house. He had always liked Heather Paul, and he had liked her father before...before what happened. Now, here he stood in this big house, battling a confusion of emotions- grief, anger, loss, fear, - and trapped into facing the man. But why? No wonder his head throbbed.

He wanted to turn and bolt out the door, but Miss Paul was already heading down a short hall to her father's office. Jamie stood rooted to the spot. I can't go in there, he thought. As if he'd spoken the words out loud, his father turned and gave him a shove. "Come on! The doctor's waitin'."

Realizing he had no choice, Jamie swore silently and marched ahead of his father. To his left, he peeked into a parlour furnished with carved furniture and a painting of a castle on one wall. He'd never seen such a fine place. It was nothing like the cramped cabins where his family and most of their neighbours lived cheek by jowl.

The colours of a patterned rug beneath his feet disoriented him. In contrast to the rough wood floors at home, its soft thickness left him strangely unbalanced. He couldn't recall ever walking on carpet before and wondered if he and his father should have removed their boots. This was a different world to his, and that realization only made him more uncomfortable.

Further down the hall, he could see into another room with a handsome table and six chairs that actually matched. The table was laid with a sparkling white cloth and already set for the next meal. Fit for a king, he thought, somewhat overwhelmed with awe and admiration for these fine objects, but at the same time surging with resentment. So unfair! Why should these people live such a nice life? His Ma had deserved nice things like this, too; she'd worked hard all her poor life, too. But she'd never have them.

Behind him his father had come to a halt beside a cabinet Jamie had failed to notice. Behind its glass doors, several intriguing items sat displayed on shelves. Heather turned around and, noting his interest, explained.

"Those are some of Father's souvenirs from the War of 1812. There were plenty of them around where we lived in Niagara."

Now, Jamie could see an assortment of guns, ammunition, Indian arrowheads, and what looked like a couple of old military caps. Everything looked pretty old and beaten up to him.

"I heard about that war," Da said. "Went back and forth for a couple o' years, didn't it?"

"Yes. The Americans invaded in 1812, and there was a lot of fighting all along our border, but in the end, they were pushed back. My father prizes this these, because his father was in that war as a young boy. I find it all a bit gruesome myself, but I guess it represents a part of our history. "

Dr. Paul must have heard their approach. He opened the door, thanked his daughter for her help, and with a sweep of his arm, invited Jamie and his father to enter.

"Take a seat, please, Ian. Jamie, there's another chair in the corner. You can bring it over here for yourself." His manner was solemn as he walked behind his desk and sat down.

Jamie couldn't move. The multiple warring thoughts and emotions tumbling around in his aching head immobilized him. He didn't want to be in that house and wished he could be just about anywhere else. *What do I do now?*

Once again, his father gave him a slight push. "What's the matter with you? Are you dreamin' again? Bring the chair over. We don't want to be wastin' the doctor's time."

Chapter Twenty

Trapped

A strange sound whooshed in Jamie's ears, as he sat down. He felt faint and closed his eyes to calm himself. It was impossible for him to look across the desk at the doctor.

"I apologize, Doctor," Ian MacGregor said, shaking his head in confusion. "I don't know what's going on. The boy's been actin' foolish for some time now."

"Yes, well..." A pause followed, as if the doctor were searching for words. The length of that pause became so unnerving, Jamie was compelled at last to look up, wondering what was going on.

To his astonishment, Dr. Paul's eyes focussed not on him, but on his father. Those eyes appeared to assess his da, as if seeing him for the first time, and in them, Jamie thought he read pity, quickly hidden by the man's usually more professional and neutral manner. Even though his father had been the focus of his own anger for some time, it was maddening to see him somehow diminished in anyone's else's sight, let alone this man's. What right did he have to judge?

"I see you noticed my collection," the doctor said, still sounding unusually formal.

Da nodded, " It's interestin'. I don't know much about that war, o' course, bein' from the old country. But your daughter says your own father was in it."

"That he was. He was just a boy, of course." Here the doctor's gaze landed on Jamie. "In fact, he was about your age. Sixteen or so. Thought it was a great adventure, until he lost a leg to cannon fire. Changed his life forever."

"Sorry to hear that, " Da said.

"Thank you."

Jamie tried to imagine himself going into battle. When he was little, he and Robbie played soldiers in the woods al the time. Sometimes, they even pretended to be shot, and they'd make a big show of falling down screaming. But then they'd always get up, laughing, and carry on. He thought about what it would be like to have a leg shot off for real.

He gave his head a shake, as if to clear his head. Why were they talking about some old war? What was the man up to? Surely, that wasn't why he'd seemed to be in such a hurry to get them here?

Dr. Paul straightened in his chair and cleared his throat. "You're probably wondering why I asked you to come, so I'll get right to the point," he said, opening a desk drawer and reaching in. "I believe I have something of yours here, Jamie." Now that not-quite-hidden note of judgement was directed at him.

"Mine?" Jamie asked in disbelief. What could this man possibly have that was his? Still, he didn't really want to know. He didn't trust him and wanted nothing to do with him. Again he closed his eyes, wishing with all his might he could avoid whatever was coming.

"My step-children found this. You'll want it back, I imagine. It is yours, I presume?"

"It sure is," he heard his father answer. "I didn't know it was lost."

This was so unexpected, Jamie looked up. His sling-shot! His mind swirled in a panic. How could it be? He knew he'd lost it somewhere, but why would Dr. Paul have it? And how could his step-children have found it? Where had they been that he'd been?

'His step-children'. The words sunk in. They were his step-children, because he'd married their mother. The wedding! Jamie knew his face was reddening. Was that really where he lost it? Outside the house? Or when he ran off? Did he drop it then, or later? He wanted to throw up.

But wait! What if it wasn't the children who found it? Maybe Dr. Paul was lying. What if someone else brought it to him? Someone who'd seen him that day. Jamie's fevered mind tried to sort through the possibilities.

"It's not mine," he said, shaking his head.

His da frowned, clearly puzzled. "Of course it is! Look at it," he insisted.

"No, it's not," Jamie insisted. "Mine's at home."

"There's a carving on it," Dr. Paul pointed out. "It reminded me of one I'd seen in your home. I was sure it was the same, and therefore, this must be yours."

"And it is," his father agreed, "It's supposed to be the MacGregor shield." He looked at Jamie, thoroughly confused by his son's denial. "What's the matter with you, boy?"

Jamie said the first thing that came into his head, "It was stolen." The words came out rushed, and his voice shook as he continued the fabrication.

"Stolen?" Da's initial surprise turned to suspicion. "When?"

"A long time ago. I didn't want to tell you. I thought you'd get mad, 'cause Grandda made it for me." The words sounded false even to his own ears.

"Don't you be lyin' now!" his father voice rose abruptly in anger. "I won't stand for any lyin'." His emotions propelled him out of his seat so that now he loomed over his son.

"I'm not." Humiliated, Jamie could barely get the words out. But before his da could reply, Dr. Paul stepped in.

"Hold on," he interjected, "Let's calm down a bit."

"But,…" Da began.

"Ian, would you mind if I spoke to Jamie alone, please?" With a tone that brooked no dissent, he added, "It might be better if you waited in the hall. Just for a minute or two."

Jamie watched the doctor's face. Once again, he was focussing on Da, this time not sure he liked what he saw.

"I don't understand. Has the boy done somethin' wrong? If there's been trouble, I want to know."

"Calm down, " Dr. Paul repeated. "Just give us a few minutes. Everything's fine."

'Fine'? What d'you mean by that? 'Everything's fine'? Jamie wanted to scream. Still keeping his head down, he heard a slight movement and knew his father had turned towards him, seeking an explanation. He could feel the anger and confusion in those pale blue eyes but couldn't look up to meet them. A rustle of clothing accompanied the creaking of the chair, as his father rose to his feet.

"Well, all right, then. I'll just be outside the door, " Da relented. But not before one last shot. "No more lyin', though, boy. If you've done somethin', own up to it."

Jamie heard a click as the door closed, and the room became quiet. Dr. Paul cleared his throat and his face visibly softened. "I'm sorry about that, but I think it's better if this is just between us now, do you agree?"

Jamie didn't respond.

"Well, I won't waste time. I think you know where this was found. And I think we both know when you lost it."

Jamie shook his head, still staring at the floor.

"Smashing a window with a rock is a pretty serious thing to do, especially with a room full of people inside, Jamie. There was glass and blood everywhere. There could have been very grave injuries; it's just luck there weren't. Yet my wife was hurt." Jamie noticed a break in the doctor's voice as he continued. "And my whole family was shaken, especially the girls."

Clearly, the doctor was distressed by what had happened to his family, and as Jamie pictured the injuries he'd caused Mrs. Paul, his heart constricted with pain. He hadn't intended to hurt her or the younger girls or Samantha. They weren't his target. He'd been so focussed on taking revenge on Dr. Paul he hadn't even thought about them. His rage had blinded him to the fact things could go so wrong. And how could he have been so stupid as to lose his slingshot there? It pointed to him as clearly as an eye-witness pointing an accusing finger.

Another lengthy pause. "I've done a lot of thinking. This wasn't an accident, or a silly prank; it was done on purpose. Somebody would have to be tremendously upset to do such a thing." A deep sigh escaped Dr. Paul's lips. "I have to wonder what made you so angry, Jamie?"

A clocked ticked somewhere out in the hall. A cough erupted nearby. Da was probably pacing back and forth out there, wondering what on earth was happening. Jamie felt miserable. Still he said nothing.

Dr. Paul continued. "You were angry enough to disrupt our wedding, so it must have been about something to do with my wife..." Dr. Paul paused, as if waiting for confirmation. "Or with me."

Now he looked at Jamie for a moment and then continued. "And I see from the look on your face it must be because of something you think I've done."

Jamie was beginning to squirm, just the littlest bit.

"You and I never met until your mother became ill. So perhaps it's about your father's reaction to that; he must be a handful." Dr. Paul watched Jamie carefully. "Or maybe this is about...your mother? Is that it?"

Suddenly Jamie leapt from his chair, knocking it over. A shocked look crossed the doctor's face, before it was replaced with an attempt at a calm appearance. Jamie saw he'd frightened the man. Good!

In one swift move, he grabbed the slingshot from Dr. Paul's hand, snapped it in two, and threw the pieces onto the desk. "You know nothing," he seethed. "I told you the damn thing was stolen."

*****

Rushing past his waiting father in the hall, Jamie took off blindly, neither knowing nor caring where he ended up, as long as it was far away from this house.

"What the...come back here!" his father's voice called after him.

The same soft carpet he'd marvelled at on his way in, now proved treacherous on his way out, as one of his boots caught on it, sending him stumbling right into the cabinet holding the doctor's collection of war souvenirs. When one of its glass doors flew open, allowing some items to tumble out to the floor, Jamie swore and kicked them out of his way, barely registering what they were, except one that looked like a horn, probably a soldier's bugle. Then he spotted an ancient pistol and without thinking, grabbed it and dashed out the front door.

"Get back here! What the hell do you think you're doin'?"

He heard his father's shouted question but knew he couldn't answer. He had no idea what he was doing. He only knew he had to keep going. Then, thud! Down he went.

*****

When Jamie landed on his backside with Caleb sitting on his chest, the gun flew out of his hand. Fighting to free himself, he couldn't believe what was happening. Hell! Just my luck! he fumed. His futile punches kept missing their mark, maddening him further.

"Let me go! I'll kill you!" he screamed.

"Try it," Caleb shouted. "I've been waiting to get my hands on you! Just give me an excuse!"

"That's enough!" A furious Mr. MacGregor broke in, hauling Jamie to his feet. "What in God's name has gotten into you?"

Caleb stood back, breathing heavily. "He's crazy, that's what." He raised a trembling hand to point straight at Jamie. "He had a gun!"

"You shut up!" Jamie wanted to lash out at all the accusing eyes staring at him. Several excited youngsters had come running to see what the commotion was about, some no doubt hoping to cheer on a good fight.

His father's face was a study in stunned disbelief. "A gun? Where'd he get a gun? What's happened to you, boy?" he demanded. When it became evident no reply was forthcoming, his expression of disbelief crumpled into one of utter hopelessness. "What have you done?" he sighed.

Dr. Paul retrieved the pistol. " It's from my collection," he told Mr. MacGregor. "He must have grabbed it on his way out."

Putting a calming hand on Caleb's shoulder, he suggested, "Let's take this back inside."

"But he…"

"Please," his step-father repeated. "Inside."

Shooting a hostile look at Jamie, Caleb acquiesced and headed for the house. An equally scathing look from his da told Jamie he'd better cooperate, too.

It was all too much. Jamie knew he didn't stand a chance, if he went back in there. "Sorry, Da," was all he could manage before he turned and ran as if his life depended on it, for in his mind, it did.

Caleb stared at his step-father in disbelief. "You just let him go? You're not going to do anything?"

"I didn't say that."

"Well, what then?"

"I need to think about this some more."

"You have to do something."

"I know. I know. But things aren't always cut and dried. That young man is a bit of a lost soul, and I don't think harsh punishment is what he needs."

"A lost soul? I don't understand you. It was my mother's wedding he tried to ruin. And yours. He's crazy, I tell you."

"You could be right, but I don't think so." Dr. Paul glanced over his shoulder to make sure Ian MacGregor was out of earshot, before resuming, "Something's very wrong here. Leave it with me. I'll handle it. And please, keep it to yourself, all right?"

Caleb respected his step-father, but he simply could not understand his thinking. In the interests of peace, he nodded his agreement and said no more. However, he remained furious and vowed to himself that Jamie MacGregor wasn't off the hook yet. He would pay for what he'd done.

Chapter Twenty-One

The Plan

Dr. Paul had a great deal on his mind, as he entered the general store and was glad to see Andrew Whylie was alone, as he'd hoped.

As always, he began with inquiries as to the state of Andrew's back. "Gettin' better, thanks to you," Andrew replied, offering the doctor chair, before settling himself on a stool behind the counter. "But it's slow. Guess I'm too impatient, but there's a lot o' lifting to do here."

"Which you know you shouldn't be doing. I wonder if you need to hire a bit of help for that?"

"Help? That would be nice, but I can't afford it."

"Well, that's up to you, of course, but maybe you can't afford not to have some. You don't want any setbacks, now that you seem to be having less pain."

"I know. I know," Andrew agreed. He seemed to ponder the idea for a moment before asking, "Did you have someone in mind? Is that why you came in?"

"Well, perhaps," the doctor admitted. "I was thinking of young MacGregor."

Andrew nodded. "Was in with his father. Seems all right. Not much to say, but he did offer to carry a load for me, which I appreciated." He smiled, "He's still young enough to have a strong back."

"Right. I don't want to push this, Andrew, but I think you'd be doing yourself a favour and the MacGregors, too." Dr. Paul stood up and paced back and forth, forming his words. "The boy's been a lost soul these past months, since his mother died." He shook his head, "His father is still grieving, too, of course, and I'm not sure he's noticed. I think there's quite a bit of anger, there, too, which concerns me. Left to his own devices, that could lead him into trouble, but at heart, I believe he's a good lad."

Andrew got off the stool and leaned against the counter to stretch his back. "And speakin' of trouble, he was here recently with that young blacksmith fella, Carr. I had a feelin' they were up to no good. Maybe going to try and steal somethin'. When I spoke to them, Carr was real cocky about it. MacGregor took off like a scared rabbit."

"I doubt Jamie'd be up to theft. I don't know Carr well enough to say one way or the other. Seems to me there's possible trouble ahead for both of them, unless somebody steps in.

"I don't know…" Considering the doctor's proposal, Andrew ran a hand over his face; his pursed lips expressed doubt. "What makes you think he'd be interested, anyway? And if he's angry about things…I don't particularly want anyone mopin' around in a black mood and drivin' customers away."

"I thought you might understand better than most." The doctor's voice was kind, when he continued, "After all, you went through a dark period yourself not so long ago." When Andrew began to protest, Dr. Paul hastened to add, "Quite understandably so. No one can blame you. But still, you carried a fair amount of resentment after your accident."

"That was completely different!"

"Maybe. Maybe not. The point is, Jamie seems to be a young man in great pain, as you were at one time. And you're only a couple of years older. Maybe he'll talk to you. At the very least, he'd be more comfortable with you than with an older person. I hope you'll give this a chance. If it doesn't work out, well, at least we tried."

Andrew felt obligated to go along with the plan. After all, he had to admit Dr. Paul was right about how angry he'd been at almost everyone not so long ago. Especially Caleb. For some reason he hadn't understood at the time, he'd had it in for Caleb Lawson. He now recognized it had been pure jealousy, because his father had hired the boy to work on the Whylie's farm.

Andrew loved that farm and his dream had been to work it with his father for the rest of his life. But a runaway log at the lumber camp one winter had smashed both his body and his dream. Fortunately, for him, Mr. and Mrs. Boyle had given him a future in this store, although he hadn't seen it that way at first. He'd been resentful and full of anger at the world. Like Jamie, he thought. And it had been Dr. Paul who had seen the hurt in him, too, and helped him crawl out of his despair.

"All right," Andrew shrugged his shoulders and sighed. "We'll give it a try. Next time I see him, I'll offer him something on Saturdays. That's our busiest day, and I could put him to work movin' supplies out of the storeroom."

"Thank you," The two men shook hands and, as Dr. Paul went out the door, he turned to add, "I don't think you'll regret this."

Watching the doctor cross the muddy street, Andrew shook his head and muttered, "Sure hope you're right."

Chapter Twenty-Two

The New Job

"You get goin' now and make sure you put in a good day's work. No complainin' now! You've brought enough shame on this family."

It was a Saturday morning, and Jamie was about to start his new job at the general store. He'd been taken aback when Andrew offered it to him. In fact, he'd asked, "Why me?" to which Andrew had replied, "Why not you? Don't you want it?"

Of course he did. He couldn't afford to turn down a chance to bring in some money. Now, he was almost looking forward to it. At least it would get him away from home for a day. His father was still very angry with him.

"You're damned lucky, you know. I don't understand exactly what's goin' on between you and Dr. Paul, but I do know you must've got yourself into some kind of trouble with damn sling-shot. He's a good man to let you go. And now Andrew's offered you a job. Just make sure you don't make him regret it. Go on now." He almost shoved his son out the door into the early morning chill.

Jamie's earlier good mood and anticipation dissolved, and now he felt so miserable he wanted to stretch out the time walking into town, but if he didn't arrive on time his whole sorry situation would be even worse. The days since his confrontation with Dr. Paul had been unbearable at home. His father was furious — at times, too furious to speak, at other times, so angry he couldn't stop giving Jamie a piece of his mind. Jamie wasn't sure which was worse.

Even Robbie had shown up to give him a tongue thrashing. "What the heck have you been up to? I'm thinkin' it had somethin' to do with that smashed window at the doc's weddin', am I right?" Jamie's guilt must have been plain to see on his face, because Robbie spat in disgust. "Does Da know?"

"No."

"Good. Let's try to keep it that way." His intense gaze examined Jamie for some sign of an explanation. "What the hell were you thinkin'?" Then he answered his own question. "I guess that's just it. You weren't thinkin' at all! What happened to that 'smart brain' of yours Ma was always goin'

160

on about." Robbie's eyes filled with sadness. "Ma!" he added. "It's a darn good thing she isn't here to see this!"

"If she was here, there wouldn't be a problem," Jamie had pointed out, almost in a whisper. He'd lost all his spit and fire. He was worn out.

"You've got to get past this, Jamie. You're not the only one who misses her. Don't you think I wish she could be here when the baby comes? She'd have loved bein' a grannie."

This thought had never crossed Jamie's mind. Robbie was right, though. Their ma would've been excited about the new baby. "I'm sorry. I didn't think…"

"You sure didn't. It's time to grow up, Jamie boy. Ma spoiled you a bit too much, you bein' the youngest and all, but you've got to straighten yourself out now."

Spoiled? Me? Robbie's words shocked Jamie. Why would Rob say that? He wanted to shout, "I'm not spoiled!", but something held him back.

His brother's face softened a little. "I know it's tough, but get this into your head once and for all – Ma was awfully sick, and Dr. Paul couldn't do anything to save her."

Not Robbie, too! Jamie hadn't wanted to fight over this. Maybe his brother and Da were right after all. But he'd held onto his anger toward Dr. Paul for o long, it wasn't easy to let it go just like that.

*****

The morning chill lingered. He shivered and swung his arms about to warm up. When the outskirts of the village appeared ahead, his steps slowed. What if he messed this up? What if Andrew decided he didn't want him after all? What if he got fired?

"You've brought enough shame on this family." His father's words sounded so clear in his head, Jamie turned around almost expecting to see him standing behind him. He knew he had no choice in the matter; he had to redeem himself, somehow. He wasn't sure he could do it, but he'd give it a shot.

"I'll try, Da. I'll try," he promised.

*****

"Time for a break," Andrew said. "Did you bring some lunch?"

"Yeah," Jamie replied, head down, reluctant to make eye contact. He was aware Andrew was staring at him.

"Anything wrong?"

"Nope."

He heard the long sigh Andrew let out. "Well, you can eat in the store room, if you like. I didn't see you bring anything in. Where is it?"

"In my jacket. There's bread 'n' cheese in the pocket."

"Good. You can help yourself to some of the milk back there, if you like."

"Thanks." Jamie turned to walk to the back of the store, still not looking up.

"You earned it. You were a big help this morning."

A slow grin spread across Jamie's face. He straightened up a bit, feeling taller, as he soaked up the compliment.

In the storeroom, he removed the package of bread and cheese from his jacket and untied the string around the paper wrapping, carefully putting the string back in his pocket 163ob e used another day. He was immediately enveloped by the cheese's strong aroma. His jacket would likely smell like it for a week.

He found the tall milk can standing in a corner. The milk smelled fresh, so he grabbed a battered cup off a nearby shelf and filled it to the brim. A quick sip confirmed the drink was both fresh and cold. Spotting a broken chair tipped over on its side, he set it upright and sat down with a deep sigh. It was a relief to get off his feet, if only briefly. He had worked hard, carrying those big barrels and crates, stocking shelves, sweeping up. He realized Andrew's words of praise meant a great deal to him.

Despite his fears, it hadn't been so bad in the store after all. He hadn't messed up. Yet! It had only been one morning. And Andrew had been decent enough.

Jamie looked around the storeroom, taking in more details. It seemed odd to be here. Before this day, he'd only been in the front part of the store as a customer. Seeing what went on from the other side was kind of interesting.

*****

"Closing time," Andrew announced. "You can go home now."

"Do you want me to come back?" Jamie still felt shy.

"You bet."

"So, next Saturday?"

"Right."

As Jamie headed out the door, Andrew called after him, "You were a big help today. Thanks."

"You're welcome." Jamie's reply was almost too soft to be heard.

Anxious to get out of the village, he kept up a brisk pace until he felt safe enough to slow down, and, almost without realizing it, began to whistle a cheerful tune.

Chapter Twenty-Three

You Can't Please Everyone

"What've you got to be whistlin' about? I heard you a mile away."

"Sorry, Da." He wondered why he was apologizing. Instinctively sniffing for signs his father had been drinking, he decided he hadn't; he was sober. Sober, and still angry.

"Well, I hope you at least put in a good day's work."

"I did. Andrew told me I did a good job."

"Well, that's somethin' anyway. Supper's on the stove. You'd best wash up."

It was a tense, quiet meal, and Jamie was glad to turn in early, but despite his fatigue, his churning thoughts kept him awake. Clearly, it was going to take more than one day of doing well at the store for his da to forgive him. He wondered how long he could take this terrible sense of loneliness.

*****

Another week passed, and the strain between the two was still great. Saturday morning, Jamie once more wrapped up some cheese and bread for his lunch and headed into town to put in another day at the store. Again, it was a relief just getting away from home for a while. He looked forward to seeing anyone other than his da for a change, even Carr . This last thought brought a rueful chuckle, as it pointed out how truly desperate he was.

"Good to see you," Andrew greeted him. This immediately made Jamie feel better. It had been a while since anyone had been glad to see him.

He nodded. "Thanks."

"Well, I've got a list of things for you to do, so let's get you started."

The morning passed in a blur of chores, but Jamie enjoyed every minute. Some customers were inclined to chat, and he found he enjoyed talking 167ot hei. One or two inquired, "Aren't you the MacGregor boy? I was awfully sorry to hear about your poor mother.", and he was able to reply without becoming too sad or angry again. He liked helping others find items they were searching for, and carrying parcels out to their wagons. In short, he was enjoying being useful and appreciated. When lunch time arrived, he was in a great mood.

"Would it be all right if I ate my lunch outside on the back steps today?" he asked. "The sun's out."

"Good idea," Andrew replied absent mindedly, his head buried in the accounts book.

*****

After settling himself on the top step, Jamie opened the package containing his lunch. He'd pulled out his pocket knife and was about to cut a piece of cheese, when the door creaked open behind him. Startled, he turned to find Andrew gazing down at him.

"Somethin' wrong?" Jamie immediately tensed.

"No. Just thought I'd join you. That sun feels good."

Jamie had been looking forward to eating alone, but what could he say? He shrugged, as if to say, "I don't care. Do what you want." It was meant to discourage Andrew without having to say anything.

"Things are slow. Decided I'd rest my bones a bit."
Andrew pulled the door shut behind him. "It's a nice day for
bein' outside."

Jamie tried not to notice Andrew's awkwardness as he
settled himself on the same step with a sigh. He can't be
much more than twenty, but sometimes he moves like an old
man, he thought. Wonder what happened? He'd heard there
was some kind of accident.

For a while, neither spoke. Jamie munched on his cheese,
and Andrew sat, eyes closed, his face to the sun.

"Feels great! Like spring. Won't be long before my father
starts planting. Him and Caleb." Another sigh followed.

Although he didn't want to talk, Jamie's curiosity got the
better of him.

"How come Caleb works for your father?"

"Well, they needed help. I can't do the work anymore.
Since my accident." Andrew lowered his head and sat, elbows
on his knees, staring at the ground.

Jamie didn't know what to say.

With one long leg, Andrew reached out and dug the toe of his boot into the ground, turning the earth over.

"Just smell that!" he said. "The ground frost is gone, and the earth's new and fresh."

Jamie'd never heard anyone get excited about dirt before.

"You like farming?" he ventured. It felt like such a stupid question, and yet, he wanted to know. He realized as Andrew spoke with such fondness about the earth and planting, that it wasn't something he himself looked forward to. It was a chore, something that had to be done, if they wanted to eat. And Da needed his help. They couldn't afford to pay hired help.

"Yeah. It's a hard life. You know that. But it's in my blood, I guess."

Again, Jamie didn't know what to say.

"But I'm not complainin'," Andrew said with a sudden smile." The Boyles were good enough to offer me this job in their store, and it's not so bad." He gave Jamie an impish wink. "Lots of pretty girls come by." A pause. "Saw you talking to the doc's step-daughter the other day when you were in with your father.

Jamie started blushing again as he remembered those embarrassing words. "Yes, you're a fine looking girl." But he'd been saying them to his horse, not her. It was his rotten luck she'd overheard, "A fine looking girl!" and misunderstood.

"Ah," Andrew chuckled. "She did catch your eye, didn't she?"

"No! I was talking to the horse, not her."

"Right." Andrew laughed again. "Well, I'll make an introduction, if you'd like."

"No!" Jamie was horrified. "Don't you dare! I'm not interested. "

"Samantha's a nice girl. I could arrange an introduction."

"Not interested!" Jamie insisted. But he was. So that's her name. Samantha. He liked the sound of it.

"We'll see," Andrew smiled. "Well, time to get back to work." He stood stiffly and took a moment to stretch his arms and legs, and turn his face to the sun again, then added, "I thought she showed some interest in you, too. At least she didn't ignore you."

Andrew went back inside, and Jamie stood to wipe the crumbs from his lunch off his shirt and pants.

"I thought she showed some interest in you," Andrew had said.

Jamie kept repeating those words to himself most of the afternoon.

*****

At home that night, tension remained. His father was still out of sorts, despite Jamie's reports about how pleased Andrew was with his work. The situation frustrated him. What more do I have to do? I've apologized a dozen times about what happened at Dr. Paul's. And he should be happy I've got a job.

With his mind full of questions, it took a long time to fall asleep that night, and the lonesome sound of a nearby wolf calling to the moon only added to his own feelings of loneliness.

Chapter Twenty-Four

Change of Plans

Something was very wrong. Jamie's da, stumbling over a chair and muttering curses, had never been drunk so early in the day. It was barely mid-morning, which meant his father must have started hitting the bottle during the night, but Jamie hadn't heard a sound. He'd been shocked to find his father in this state, and now he didn't know what to do. Leave him alone? Try to wrestle the bottle out of his hands? He had to admit he was a bit scared.

"What are you starin' at? You git on yer way." The anger in those slurred words hurt.

"I don't have to go in to the store today, Da." Jamie fought to keep his voice calm.

"Don't talk back! I told you before, Robbie's needin' a bit o' help. You'll head on over and give him a hand."

"What's he need me for?" He didn't remember any talk about Robbie needing help, and he also knew he shouldn't challenge his da in this state, but the question tumbled out anyhow.

"Just get on your damn way," his father muttered. "No need for so many blasted questions."

Jamie bit his tongue, wanting to keep the peace. It occurred to him his father might simply want him out of the way for a while, and that thought hurt.

He grabbed his jacket and headed out the door. Although he wanted to slam it behind him, he took care not to.

*****

He found his brother, axe in hand, at the woodpile.

"Thought I'd do you a favour and get you away for a few hours," Robbie greeted him. "I know how Da can be when he's angry. Although, I have to give him some credit. He hasn't been drinkin' so much lately."

Jamie couldn't believe it. Robbie had been trying to help him. How great was that? He tried to smile. He could relax here and forget about Da for a while; his brother wouldn't bite his head off at every turn.

"Thanks." Even to his own ears, his reply sounded feeble, lacking the enthusiasm he'd intended, and Robbie was quick to notice. Damn!

"What's wrong? The old man still giving you a hard time?" Robbie straightened up, shifting the axe in his hand.

Jamie made a show of looking around the clearing. "Give me something to do." He'd managed more enthusiasm this time and even an attempt at humour. "It sure looks like you need a lot of help. A lot."

"Oh, I've got a long list, but you haven't answered me. Is Da still givin' you a hard time?"

Jamie avoided Robbie's eyes, not wanting to see the inevitable disappointment in them. "He's at it again, Rob. I've never seen him like this so early in the day. Must have started in the middle of the night this time."

"Shit! When's this going to stop? He's being an ass."

The harsh words shocked Jamie so much, he actually tried to defend his father. "It's all since Ma died."

"Not good enough. He's got responsibilities like the rest of us, and if he keeps this up, he'll be the next one in the grave." The axe landed hard in a stump, as Robbie turned and stomped off towards the house. "Come on," he called over his shoulder.

Jamie followed, confused. Was it lunch time already?

*****

"Well, at least have your lunch first," Melinda was saying to Robbie as Jamie came through the door.

"No. I'm not stopping until I talk some sense into him. This has got to stop."

"Well, at least let me pack some of it up for you to take with you."

For the first time, Melinda seemed to notice Jamie, who had tried to shrink into a corner out of their way.

"Jamie," was all she said, with a slight nod, Then, looking from one brother to the other, she asked, "What do you think you can do? If your father's drunk, there's really no point..."

"I can't let this go on any longer," Robbie said. "Come on, Jamie."

"No, Robbie," Jamie stood in the doorway, blocking his brother's way. "It'll only make things worse. Forget it. I'll stay here and work with you, and by the time I get back, he'll be over it. He'll probably be asleep."

"He's right You should stay here," Melinda agreed, but she could see Robbie wasn't listening; he was determined to go. "Wait, then," she pleaded, pointing to the food she had put out for lunch. "I'll pack up some of this and come with you. It'll just take a minute."

Robbie began to protest, and Jamie interrupted. "I really don't think that's a good idea, Melinda..."

But she was already gathering up bread and cheese and a jar of pickles. "Food always helps," she declared, "Besides, your father's more likely to behave if I'm there. I'm coming, and that's all there is to it. Help me with this pot of soup, please. It's hot."

Jamie watched the conflicting emotions play out on his brother's face. He could tell Robbie knew Melinda might be a help, but he also didn't want to put her through all this unpleasantness. It only took a moment for him to decide, however. "All right, but in that case, we'll take the wagon."

Heading out the door, he said, "Come on, Jamie, we'll hitch up Blackie."

Jamie glanced at Melinda bustling around and looking quite pleased with herself. He had a sudden, sick premonition and wished with all his heart he'd kept his mouth shut.

Chapter Twenty-Five

Crisis

"Well, what a nice shur...shur...prise!" Da clung to the door in an effort to hold himself upright but began to lose his grip and slide towards the floor.

Robbie grabbed his father and shoved him into a chair with unaccustomed roughness. "Take it easy!' His father moaned, as his head dropped forward and his chin came to rest on his chest. His eyes began to close, but Robbie startled him awake, shouting in his face, "Wake up!"

"Rob, don't, please." Melinda put a gentle hand on him arm. "Let me." Stepping between the two men, she held up the basket of food to show her father-in-law. "We've brought lunch, Mr. MacGregor. "There's fresh bread and soup I think you'll like. I'll just heat it up on the stove."

Amazed, Jamie watched his father calm down and bestow an unfocussed smile on Melinda. "B...bless you, m' dear."

Melinda returned his smile, and glanced at both Jamie and Robbie, as if to say, "See? I was right."

Except for an occasional noisy burp from Mr. MacGregor, and a short-lived attempt at cheerful chatter from Melinda, a depressing silence descended on the cabin. Jamie, unable to bear the scene, kept his eyes on the floor.

Sometime later, a slight groan caused him to lift his head. He knew it hadn't come from his da.

Melinda, looking pale and frightened, sat rocking back and forth in a chair, her arms wrapped around herself in a tight embrace.

"What's wrong?" Robbie cried, his voice full of alarm. Kneeling beside her, he placed a hand on her damp forehead and brushed aside a stray lock of hair. "You don't look right. What is it?"

"Oh, Robbie." Her voice was a hoarse whisper. "Something's wrong. I'm scared."

"Are you in pain? When did this start?" The rapid questions poured out. "Oh, my God. Is it the baby?"

"I've had some twinges the past couple of days. But it wasn't too bad, and it went away, so I didn't say anything. I figured that's probably normal. But now..." She stopped, a look of horror on her perspiring face, "Oh, dear God! Look!" she pointed to her skirt. "There's blood! I'm bleeding!"

Robbie jumped to his feet so quickly he nearly lost his balance. "Hold on! I'll get Mrs. Crowley. She'll know what to do." He looked around the room. It was only then that he and Jamie both noticed their father had passed out completely. He hadn't heard a thing. Such a look of disgust crossed Robbie's face, it was painful for Jamie to see.

Robbie turned to Jamie. "You take care o' Melinda!"

Before Jamie could reply, Melinda cried, "Mrs. Crowley's gone to her daughter's in Bracebridge. She won't be back for a week."

"How could she do that?" Robbie's voice rose in panic. "She's the midwife! She should be here!" He pulled at his hair with both hands, as if yanking on it would help him think.

"Don't be upset. I'm not due for a few months. She doesn't have to stick around for me." Melinda winced and clasped her stomach. She gave Robbie a panicked look. "I think I should lie down."

Jamie didn't know what to do or say. This was private stuff between Robbie and Melinda, and he didn't want to be in the way, but where could he go?

Robbie scooped Melinda up in his arms and headed toward Da's bedroom, unaware of a burning smell which caught Jamie's attention. Rushing to the stove, he grabbed a scorched pot off the burner and immediately dropped it. It landed on the floor with an immense clatter and rolled across the room. *Oh, God. Not again! Not again! Idiot!*

"Damn!" He stuck his burned fingers in his mouth to ease the intense pain and danced around in a tight circle. "Damn, damn, damn, damn, damn!"

"What the hell's goin' on now?" Robbie's angry voice shouted from the bedroom. "Jamie?"

"Sorry! The soup was burning. I took it off the stove. But I dropped it. Sorry!" There was no reply.

Robbie stomped out of the bedroom. He didn't notice the overturned pot and the mess on the floor. He didn't appear to see Jamie, either. His wild eyes searched the walls and ceiling of the cabin for something. Whatever it was, they didn't seem to find it.

"I've got to do something," Robbie whispered. "This isn't good. She's so pale."

"Can I go and find someone to help, a neighbour maybe?" ~~He~~ *Jamie* searched his mind for a name. "What about Mrs. Whylie, Andrew's mother?"

"No. Too far." ~~Andrew's~~ *Robbie's* quick response was emphatic. Straightening with resolve, he announced, " Has to be Dr. Paul. We need a real doctor. Especially with the midwife gone."

Without thinking, Jamie blurted out, "Not Dr. Paul, Robbie. Please, don't."

Robbie yelled, "Yes, Dr. Paul. Get that into your thick head. Dr. Paul is our best chance, so just stop!"

He stared Jamie into silence. "All right. Now, I'm goin' to tell Melinda I'm going for the doc, and you'll be right here if she needs you."

As Robbie returned to the bedroom, Jamie panicked, his thoughts racing. Stay alone with Melinda? When she was like this? No! He couldn't. He looked at his da, wanting to scream, "Wake up! We need you! Don't you give a damn?" Instead, he wound up and kicked the leg of the man's chair, eliciting nothing more than a noisy snort from his da but an agonizing pain shooting through his own foot.

After a brief, whispered conversation in the bedroom, Robbie emerged and grabbed his jacket.

"Wait! I'll go," Jamie insisted. "It's better if you stay with Melinda." He was still desperate to leave, so desperate he was even willing to go fetch Dr. Paul.

"No, I need to go. The doc could be hard to find. He could be anywhere." As he headed for the door, Robbie added, "I'll unhitch Blackie 'n throw a saddle on 'er. It'll be faster."

Jamie gave it one last try, "I could take her."

"She'd throw you off in a minute," Robbie scoffed. "You'd break your neck. You know she won't let anyone else on her."

Perhaps sensing his younger brother's panic, he turned and lay a hand on his shoulder. "You can do this," he said. After a brusque glance at their father, he looked Jamie in the eyes. "Da's not going to be of any use. I need to count on you."

Before Jamie could protest again, Robbie was off to get his horse.

Chapter Twenty-Six

Alone

For a long minute, Jamie stood in the doorway watching his brother try to get a halter on Blackie before throwing on a saddle. The horse, sensing her owner's tension, turned in circles, kicking out her back legs. "Settle down! Settle down!" Robbie tried to calm her, lowering his voice to a soothing cadence. "Settle down. That's a good girl!"

The words brought an image to Jamie's mind. He remembered saying something similar to Da's horse, Annie, just the other day outside the general store. And he remembered the pretty girl with bouncing curls who'd stopped to smile at him, as if she thought he was talking to her. His face grew warm with embarrassment, remembering the scene. What a dolt he'd been. He must've looked like an idiot, talking to a horse like that. She'd surely told all her friends about it by now! And now he knew she was Dr. Paul's step-daughter, Samantha, he felt even worse.

"Jamie?" Melinda called, startling him. "I'm terribly cold. Is the door open?"

"Sorry!" He hurried to shut it. "I was watching Robbie go. I'll close it."

"Thank you." The weakness in her voice struck him. He knew it wasn't a good sign.

As his hand pushed the door shut, the throbbing pain in his burned fingers made him gasp. Biting down on his lip helped him stifle any other cries or sounds. He didn't want to scare Melinda. She didn't need anything else to worry about.

Grabbing a corner of his untucked shirt, he wrapped it tightly around the red fingers, applying pressure, which seemed to ease the pain.

The cabin was quiet, except for the occasional hiss and crackle of wood burning in the stove. Even his father lay still. *As still as death*, he thought and was unprepared for the rising panic in his chest, which calmed only when he became aware of a slight widening of his da's nostrils every few seconds. Jamie, too, remained motionless. It was as if his body couldn't remember how to move, or his brain how to direct his body.

A long moment passed in this manner, until he noticed an acrid smell - the pot of soup he'd dropped. Fortunately, it had remained almost upright, and most of the contents were still in it. Picking it up, he sniffed. It smelled all right, so maybe some of it could be rescued. Eating didn't appeal to him right now, but it might later, when Robbie got back. He hoped that would be soon. But when he did return, Dr. Paul would be with him, and Jamie didn't want to be around. Didn't want to see him, if he didn't have to; the memory of their last meeting still haunted hi. Maybe he could slip out when he heard them on the road. Melinda would be all right alone for a few minutes. So, he had a plan: as soon as he heard them approaching, he'd head for home.

*****

Busying himself cleaning up the floor, Jamie tried not to dwell on Melinda and what might happen to her. He didn't want to deal with such momentous possibilities. As he listened for any sounds from the bedroom, he prayed she was asleep and would stay that way until Robbie got back.

For the first time in his life, he also prayed his father would remain quietly passed out. The idea of Da awake and thundering about was just one more possibility he didn't want to deal with.

"Jamie?"

Damn! "Yes?" He tried to make his voice sound normal and crossed his fingers, hoping Melinda wouldn't want anything. He didn't know what he could do for her. He didn't know anything about ladies having babies! "Please, God. Let her fall asleep," he whispered.

But it was not to be. "Could I have a drink?" Melinda's voice sounded so different, almost like a little girl's. "Please?" She was not her usual self. Jamie found the change unsettling.

"Sure," he replied, trying to sound more confident than he felt.

On a ledge near the stove, sat the usual pail of water with its tin cup hooked over the rim. Thank goodness he didn't have to go out for water and leave Melinda alone. Scooping deep into the pail, he filled the cup to the brim and, holding it in nervous, trembling hands, took slow, deliberate steps past his father to the bedroom.

It had been several months since he'd been in his parents' old room, the one where his mother had died, and it required even more courage than he might have imagined to enter. Still, he managed to do so for Robbie's sake. *And Melinda's*, he reminded himself.

As he might have guessed, it was no longer the tiny refuge his mother had kept neat and clean. Though only a faint light filtered through the dirt-caked window, it was enough to see the jumble of dirty bedding and stinking clothes his father had allowed to take over. Melinda lay on top of the pile of bedding. In the dimness, he searched for a place to set the cup down.

"It stinks in here. I'll let some air in," he said, turning to the window.

"No. It's too cold out." Melinda pointed to the cup. "Would you hold it for me, please? While I have a sip?"

He nodded and approached the bed, frightened by how pale she looked. When he noticed she could barely raise her head, he became more alarmed than ever.

"Here," he said, bending over her, "I'll help you sit up a bit." Despite his nervousness, he put his left arm under her shoulders and helped raise her up enough to take the sip. Instead, she took several big gulps, then choked and spewed water all over his shirt.

"Oh, I'm sorry!" As if the effort of raising her head and drinking had been too much, Melinda's body slumped, and

Jamie helped her lie back down. "Thank you," she said. "I'm so thirsty. I don't know why. Maybe it's this headache that's started."

"I better let you have a rest now." As Jamie straightened up, Melinda grabbed his free hand in a fierce grip. "Stay. Please!"

His heart thudded with renewed panic. "You should sleep. I'll just be in the next room."

"No! Don't leave me alone!" Melinda's voice was suddenly stronger, and her eyes pleaded with him. "Please," she continued in a whisper.

"All right," he agreed, and started to move across the tiny room to a chair against the wall, but Melinda wouldn't let go of her fierce grip. With a moan and an effort, she shifted over slightly and indicated he should sit on the edge of the bed.

Jamie was horrified. He didn't want to sit on this bed and hold Melinda's hand. *Robbie, where are you? What's taking so long?*

He looked towards the tiny window, as if he might catch sight of his brother and Dr. Paul hurrying back to the rescue. However, he had to acknowledge that, even if he could have seen through all the dirt, it was too soon. Then a horrible thought took hold. What if Dr. Paul wasn't home? What if Robbie had to go chasing all over looking for him? That could take hours and hours.

In utter despair, Jamie sank down on the edge of the bed, placing the half-empty cup of water on the floor. In order for him to do so, Melinda had to release his hand, and he let out a deep sigh of relief. Too soon! The next instant, he almost cried out in agony as she grabbed hold of his burned hand. She didn't seem to notice him flinch, however, and before he could say anything, she whispered, "I'm so scared."

This was a different Melinda, far from the strong, pushy person he knew. And if she was scared, he was terrified

Chapter Twenty-Seven

What Makes a Grown-Up?

Jamie's burned fingers throbbed, and his right arm was getting all pins and needles from being held in the same position for what seemed like hours. He knew it had only been about fifteen minutes, but those few minutes now counted among the longest of his life. Sweat beaded on his forehead from the excruciating pain.

Stealing a sideways glance at Melinda, he noted her closed eyes, but he was sure she wasn't fully asleep. Still, he didn't dare try to extricate himself from her grasp, which thankfully had relaxed somewhat. Holding onto him seemed to have calmed her. This unexpected revelation amazed him. He wasn't certain what was going on, but he had to admit it felt pretty good. Maybe it was the idea of helping someone in trouble. Even if it was Melinda! Immediately, he regretted the thought. Melinda was in a bad way.

A strange idea occurred to him: the idea that he was feeling a little bit proud of himself. Proud he was helping Robbie and Melinda. He shook his head in disbelief.

Lately, he hadn't paid much attention to those ideas about helping others or doing good deeds. When his mother was alive, she'd always encouraged him to be the best he could be, but then she died and everything changed.

"Maybe it's time for you to grow up," Robbie had told him the other day. But Jamie's mind had rebelled. Who wants to grow up?

Now he asked himself what that meant anyway. He was almost seventeen. In his mind, he was already a grown-up! Deep down, however, he knew being a grown-up meant much more than just your age.

Melinda turned over on the bed, but he pretended not to notice.

"Jamie? Thank you for staying. I know you didn't want to."

"Sure, I did," he lied. He'd been telling more than a few lies lately, but surely there must surely be times when that was all right? Like when you don't want to hurt someone's feelings, he reasoned.

In response, Melinda squeezed his hand again. "Ow-w-w!" he cried before he could stop himself. She immediately let go, and he flapped his hand around to distract himself from the pain.

"What is it? What's wrong with your hand?" Melinda demanded. "Let me see."

Jamie hid his hand behind his back. "It's nothing."

"Don't lie to me, Jamie MacGregor. Something's wrong. Let me see it."

"I burned it a little on the soup pot, that's all. It'll be fine."

"Let me see it, Jamie! You can't fool around with burns. They can get infected."

Jamie could see Melinda becoming agitated. She struggled to sit up. He needed to do something to calm her down again.

"Don't try to get up! I'll show it to you." He removed his hand from behind his back. "Here, look. It's just a bit red, see? And it doesn't hurt so much anymore." He hoped he'd sounded convincing. "Now, you'd better lie down."

"It's starting to blister. That's not good." Melinda flopped back down on the bed, as if the talking had exhausted her. "I'm sure your ma kept a jar of ointment somewhere. Maybe in the drawer in the sideboard? Have a look and if it's there, I'll dress your hand. And we'll need a clean cloth to wrap it up."

"But…"

"Don't argue, Jamie, please. I'm too tired. Just look for the ointment." She pointed to the dresser across the room. "Maybe you'll find some clean cloths in there amongst your ma's old things."

He didn't argue any further. Instead, he returned to the main room, tiptoeing past his father once again, and opened the sideboard gently so it wouldn't squeak. Melinda was right. He'd forgotten the jar of ointment, but it was still there.

In the bedroom, he obeyed her directions again and pulled open a dresser drawer to search for a clean cloth. The jolt of emotions brought on by the familiar sight and scent of his mother's clothes nearly took his knees out from under him. He should have known better. Damn it, Melinda should have known better than to ask him to do this.

"Forget it!" he started to slam the drawer shut, but something he'd never seen before caught his eye. Something so delicate and tiny, he blinked and looked twice.

"What is it? What's wrong?" Melinda sensed his hesitancy.

"I don't know," he said in a softer tone, wiping his hands on his trousers before touching the silky, white item. It looked like a piece of clothing that would fit one of the fairy-folk his mother described in her stories.

"Jamie? What is it?"

What in God's name was he thinking? Fairy-folk! Complete nonsense.

Giving his head a shake, he grabbed the item and almost threw it at Melinda. "Here, you can tear a strip off this. It looks clean enough."

In the dim light, Melinda held up the cloth. "Oh!" she gasped, and to Jamie's dismay, her eyes filled with tears. "We can't use this!" she declared.

"Why not? It's clean. I thought that's what you wanted."

The look he received was one of astonishment. " Don't you know what this is?" she asked in a hushed, almost reverential tone, as if speaking about some holy relic. What was she going on about?

"No. I've never seen it before," he replied, taking another, more careful look. "What is it?"

"It's a Christening gown, for heaven's sake! For a baby." Her voice filled with wonder. "It must've been Robbie's. And yours, of course. Just think, your ma kept it all these years."

Jamie was quite sure neither he nor his brother had ever worn anything so fancy, but what else could it be? Melinda must be right. Still, why would his ma keep it all these years? She didn't have any more children.

"Maybe she hoped for a grandchild some day," Melinda said, as if reading his mind. "It's like a sign, isn't it? A sign that everything's going to be all right."

Her eyes now shone with such hope that Jamie could only nod in agreement. Up until now, the idea of a baby hadn't seemed real, but looking at that tiny garment his mother must have sewed, he realized it was very real indeed.

He sneaked a quick look out the window, hoping to see a horse or buggy trotting up the road. So strong was his disappointment, his whole body slumped. Not a soul was in sight. Help, if it was coming could be a long way off.

He attempted to buoy his spirits by convincing himself Melinda was right and finding the gown really was a good sign. The most important thing now was keeping her safe, for Robbie's sake, and with his da still passed out, that was up to him now. Jamie had never felt so alone.

Chapter Twenty-Eight

A Startling Story

"It's too soon for Robbie to be back."

Darn! Melinda had seen him looking out the window. Jamie swore to himself. He hadn't wanted to worry her.

"Even if Dr. Paul's at home," she continued, "It could be another hour before they get...,Oh, no! Here it comes again! " Grabbing her stomach, she groaned with the sudden pain.

When the moment passed, Melinda's forehead was covered in perspiration, and she looked even more pale than before. "If he's not there..."

"Don't you worry. He will be." More softly, as if speaking to himself, he added, "He has to be."

*****

Melinda told him how to apply the smelly, green ointment. "You don't need much," she warned. "A little bit goes a long way."

"That's good, 'cause it stinks!" he blurted out. "Sorry!" he rushed to apologize. "I didn't mean to say that."

"No, you're right. It does stink." Melinda actually smiled. "My mother used to make the same concoction. She put it on everything, blackfly bites, rashes, burns, even broken bones!" She laughed at a memory. "She put it on the dog once when he got porcupine quills in his snout! The poor thing ran off and rolled in mud, trying to get rid of the smell."

Jamie struggled with one of the cloths he'd ripped from an old apron, attempting to secure it around his hand, but he couldn't help smiling at the image, too.

"Here, let me do that," Melinda offered. "I've got two hands." She patted the side of the bed. "Sit here."

Jamie obeyed and watched as his sister-in-law tore the cloth into narrower strips and expertly wound them around his blistered fingers with great gentleness. A memory came to him of the day she'd slapped salve on the his bite from the piglet. This Melinda seemed like a different person.

When she'd finished, he thanked her. "You're welcome," she replied. "But I'm the one who should be thanking you. I don't know what I'd do without you." Her warm smile so discombobulated him, that he blurted out, "I didn't think you liked me."

"Where on earth did you get that idea? Of course, I do." Melinda's face registered her confusion.

" I don't know. It's just that lately...you seemed different. I thought you were mad at me. or something."

"Oh, Jamie, no!" She shook her head. "I'm sorry you felt that way." Her eyes looked off as if she were seeing something in the distance. When she spoke again, her voice was barely a whisper. "I guess I've just been scared lately, that's all."

Melinda was scared. Of him? This was too much for his mind to absorb or figure out. He was terrified to ask but knew he had to. "Are you scared of me?"

"Of you? Oh, dear, no! No, no, never!"

Her words reassured him, but he didn't like to think she was still frightened of something. How far should he push this, though?

Melinda seemed to struggle for words. "I guess the truth is I've been scared of having this baby. It's silly, I know, but I've never done this before, and I know sometimes things don't go well, and so…"

Jamie felt like a fish out of water. He didn't know what to do. This was something he knew nothing about. *Where is everybody?* his mind screamed. *Why aren't they here yet?*

"Everything's going to be fine," he said with more conviction than he felt. "The doctor's on his way." When she didn't respond, he tried a bit of desperate humour. "I'm sure glad I didn't rip up that Christening gown. I didn't even know what the darn thing was. But since Robbie and I have obviously outgrown it, now you can have it for your baby."

He waited for a smile which didn't come. "I just hope there'll still be a baby." Melinda said, laying her hands on her stomach and turning her face away, but not before Jamie noticed fresh tears forming.

Now, he was at a complete loss for words.

"I miss my mother," Melinda whispered. "She had a cure for everything. Like that smelly ointment. But she always knew what to do." Jamie couldn't remember Melinda's mother. She'd died when he was little.

Melinda shifted slightly on the bed, trying to get more comfortable, then added, "I miss your mother, too. She was so good. Especially at times like this."

He realized he didn't know anything about how his ma and Melinda had got along, because he'd never paid attention, but her words intrigued him.. "What do you mean, 'especially at times like this'?" he asked.

"You know. When there's a baby coming. When she was a mid-wife."

"Ma was a mid-wife?" He'd never heard that before! "My Ma?

"Don't tell me you didn't know! Your mother delivered a lot of babies around here, including my younger sister. Most folks say she was wonderful at it, too. It's too bad she stopped."

"I never heard any of this." He was truly astounded. He thought he knew pretty much everything about his parents, especially his mother. "She must have stopped when I was really young. I don't remember anything about it."

"I guess that's right. You'd have been too young."

"Why'd she stop, if she was so good at it?"

"I don't know. I was only a little girl then, too."

Jamie considered this new information about his mother. "Doesn't sound like Ma. She wasn't a quitter, especially if people needed her."

"No, she wasn't," Melinda agreed. "Later on I did hear something. I don't believe it, though. You know how people like to talk." She stopped, as if regretting her words.

"What? What did you hear? Tell me!"

Melinda sighed. "I heard something went wrong once or twice, and people blamed her. It's nonsense, of course, Sarah was the most careful and conscientious person I know. If something did go wrong, it wouldn't have been her fault."

Melinda's story left Jamie dumbfounded. The whole idea of his mother being a mid-wife was new to him. He knew he shouldn't be so surprised; she'd been kind and always helpful when someone was sick. But the rest of the story! He shook his head in disbelief at the idea something had gone wrong and people blamed his Ma. That couldn't be right. Not his Ma.

"But that's not fair!" he protested.

"No, it's not," Melinda sighed. "And now she's gone, too." She paused and attempted a smile. "Look at us. We're a poor motherless pair. I guess we're going to have to be the grown-ups now. Especially me, when the baby comes."

*****

Late in the afternoon, Jamie stood at the window staring out in the gathering dusk. Still no sign of Robbie or Dr. Paul. Melinda had finally fallen asleep, for which he was grateful. He was also grateful they'd talked about why her behaviour seemed to have changed. She wasn't mad at him, after all. She was scared. That thought had never occurred to him.

He thought about what she'd said about the two of them being the grown-ups now. Melinda was only a couple of years older than he was, but she was going to be a mother, if all went well. If all went well. The words kept repeating in his mind. *If all went well.*

Chapter Twenty-Nine

Robbie Returns

Ouch! A sharp pain in his hand caused Jamie to wince. He swore when he saw blood. He hadn't even realized he'd been biting his fingernails and now one was bleeding. Sticking the throbbing finger in his mouth, he found sucking on it oddly comforting. In the last hour or so, fear and loneliness had arisen, which likely explained the nail biting.

He thought of Melinda's much more serious pain. He was doing his best to comfort and help her and hoped it would be enough for both her and the baby she and Robbie were so excited about.

The weight of this heavy responsibility had settled into an ache in his neck and shoulders. He thought of his own mother, the midwife, and wondered what she would have done, if she were here. Earlier, when Melinda had been unable to get comfortable, he'd had a sudden memory of something he'd seen his mother do from time to time. So, he'd placed a couple of rolled up blankets under her feet to take some pressure off her back, and to his relief, she said it helped. He was rather pleased and allowed himself a small smile of satisfaction. It occurred to him now that perhaps, in a way, his ma had been there in the room with them after all.

*****

Every bone in Jamie's body felt stiff. He stood up to stretch, then without a sound, slipped out of the bedroom and closed the door behind him. The main room was much colder, as the fire had died down a bit, but the chill hadn't woken his father, who still appeared to be in a deep sleep.

Taking great care not to waken his da, he moved past him and began to stoke the fire. Once it was going well, he decided to fill the kettle and start it boiling for tea. Once that was done, he decided he could sit down for the short wait, but when he took a seat opposite his father at the table, his fatigue caught up to him at last, and he couldn't resist laying his head down on his arms. He assured himself everything would be all right; it was only for a minute or two, and he'd keep one eye open to watch the kettle.

*****

Jamie jolted upright and caught himself slipping off his chair. Annoyed he'd fallen asleep, he immediately rose to check the stove, where the kettle boiled away, emitting plumes of steam. Thank heavens he'd woken before it boiled dry.

Across from him, his father slept on, head and arms resting on the table. He seemed peaceful, except for the times when an occasional, thunderous snore caused his entire body to shake. For the first time, Jamie noticed the thinning hair on the top of his father's head and saw him, not as the strong person he'd always known, but as a more frail man worn down by life and the loss of his wife.

How long had they dozed, he wondered? The lunch Melinda had brought still lay cold and untouched on the table before him. He tore off a chunk of bread and chewed on it. His movements, quiet as they were, caused his father to yawn and open his eyes. When they began to close again, as if to go back to sleep, Jamie wished he'd stay awake and talk to him. He was about to say so, when a loud thud and crash in the bedroom brought both of them to their feet, rushing towards the sound.

*****

Melinda lay on the floor. "I'm sorry! I just needed to get up for a bit. I guess I tripped over my shoes on the floor there."

Da pushed past Jamie and, attempting to kneel down, almost fell on top of Melinda. "What's goin' on? Are you all right, lass? Have you hurt yourself?"

Jamie didn't give her a chance to answer. "What were you trying to do? You know you should stay in bed until the doctor gets here."

"But I needed to get up. And the pain hasn't been too bad for a little while."

"Still, you shouldn't have tried to move. You can call for anything you need, and I'll bring it." He knew he sounded angry, and he was, but not with Melinda, with himself---angry and guilty for having fallen asleep. Robbie had trusted him to keep an eye on Melinda, and he'd failed. "Are you sure you didn't hurt yourself?"

"Yes. Truly. I'm all right. Thank you." Melinda struggled to sit up.

"Wait, dear. Let us give you a hand. We'll all feel better if you'll get back into bed."

Once Melinda settled, her feet propped up on the two blankets again, Da patted her hand. "The kettle's boilin'. D'you fancy a cup o'…."

The door flew open and Robbie rushed in with Dr. Paul on his heels.

Robbie's wild eyes raced from Melinda's relieved face to Jamie's and his father's startled ones.

"What's going on? Is everything all right? Melinda?" He moved forward and took hold of her hands. Jamie moved aside, bumping into his father. The tiny room was overcrowded and suffocating.

"Out! All of you." Dr. Paul's stern voice caught everyone's attention. He stood in the doorway, black bag in hand.

"But...," Robbie protested.

"I said, all of you. Now." The doctor's manner was firm. "There isn't room to swing a cat in here."

The three MacGregor men almost tripped over each other in their haste to get out of the tiny bedroom. "Of course, Doctor." "Thank you, Dr. Paul." "I'm glad you're here." Their collective relief was obvious in their faces, which now looked less strained than they had for several hours.

As Dr. Paul offered his patient a reassuring smile, he commented, "I'm sure Melinda needs some breathing room, right, my dear? It is rather stuffy in here."

Placing his black bag on the bed, he turned and closed the door on the others.

*****

Robbie paced the room, while Jamie and his father sat at the table.

"Sit down, son. It's not helping, and you'll wear a hole in the floor."

"I can't sit down!" Robbie almost shouted. "Not until I know she's all right. And I don't need any advice from you. Jamie, what happened while I was gone?"

"Not much." He was grateful Robbie hadn't seen Melinda lying on the floor a short while ago and felt miserable that he'd let his brother down by dozing off. "She mostly slept."

"Well, at least that sounds good. She didn't have too much pain?"

"She said it was a bit better."

"That's good, too."

"Where did you find the doctor? Was he at home?"

"No. But thank God, he wasn't far away, just at the Boyles. Mr. Boyle is ill."

"I'm sorry to hear that," his father replied, with a heavy sigh. "If anything happens to him, Mrs. Boyle will be quite lost."

Distracted by his own worries, Robbie didn't reply.

"She's got Andrew running the store," Jamie put in. He didn't know what that had to do with anything. He just wanted to say something, anything, to distract Robbie from his constant worrying about Melissa.

"It's no the same thing at all," his da commented. "Andrew's her employee. Mr. Boyle has been her husband for many, many years." For a moment, his mind seemed to be far away, and a sadness clouded his eyes. "Someday, you'll understand."

Jamie wondered yet again if he would ever get anything right. Now he'd only succeeded in reminding Da of his own loss. He got up and paced the floor like Robbie. His father, lost in thought, didn't seem to notice.

Chapter Thirty

Diagnosis

All eyes turned to the bedroom door as Dr. Paul came out. Jamie tensed; he still felt agitated and awkward in the doctor's presence. He probably always would, and that last time in the man's office, when he'd been confronted with his slingshot, hadn't helped.

Robbie's voice almost squeaked with emotion, as he demanded, "Is everything all right?" Jamie was taken aback to see his brother on the verge of tears.

"Everything should be fine, as long as she stays off her feet for a while," Dr. Paul tried to reassure Robbie as he closed the door behind him. "I'm not happy about the bleeding. That's why I want her to have some bedrest. As for the pain, I explained to Melinda that women in her condition sometimes experience this. It's caused by the baby stretching the ligaments in her stomach as it grows."

He looked at Robbie, "Do you understand? It's the growing baby causing pressure."

Robbie took in this information. "So, it's normal?"

"That part is," Dr. Paul continued. "But not the bleeding. Most of the time, these pains are reasonably mild, but hers seem to be a bit more intense. I'm sure she was frightened, not knowing what was happening. After all, this is her first. But she's young and healthy, and so far, everything's been going along as it should. Just make sure she stays off her feet for at least a week, and let me know right away if there's any more bleeding."

Robbie nodded. "I'll see to it she stays in bed."

"Good. And once she starts getting up again, she should take things slowly, not too many sudden movements. That could bring on the pain again. She must move slowly when she gets out of bed, for example, or even out of a chair." He smiled. "But with the weather warming up, it will be good for her to get outside a bit. Fresh air's the best tonic."

Relief was written all over Robbie's face. He shook the doctor's hand, thanking him over and over again.

He turned to his father and brother. "Everything's fine," he repeated, as if they hadn't been right there listening.

Like a horrible, dark presence that had held them captive for hours, the tension in the room evaporated. It was as if someone had pulled back the curtains on a window to flood the room with sunlight and set them free.

Dr. Paul pulled out a chair and sat down with a weary slump. Noticing this, Jamie's da asked, "How about some tea, doctor? You look tired. Thank you for coming out so late."

"Thanks, Ian. Tea would go down well right now."

Da attempted to rise from his chair, but stumbled, unsteady on his feet.

"I'll do it," Robbie said, disgust written all over his face. "You're in no condition to do anything."

Da plopped back down in his seat, silent and chastened. Dr. Paul pretended not to notice, but Jamie was sure he hadn't missed a thing. He tried to cover up the embarrassing moment by pointing out, "The kettle's already boiled, Rob. I put it on just a short while ago."

He remembered his original plan to get away from the cabin, as soon as he heard Robbie and the doctor approaching. Well, that hadn't worked; he'd missed the sounds of their arrival, because he'd been in the bedroom helping Melinda. Maybe now he could make an excuse to leave, go anywhere, even if it was only out to the barn. He'd be warm enough with the animals. Anything would be better than staying in this cabin with all the bad feelings. Melinda was going to be all right. They didn't need him.

While Robbie busied himself at the stove, the doctor yawned and rubbed his eyes. Soon, they closed, and his chin dropped to his chest, as if he'd drifted off to sleep. No one spoke, allowing the man to rest. Jamie made his move.

Standing up, he half-whispered, "I should check on things in the barn." Neither his brother nor his father responded; each one lost in his own world. "Fine, then," he said to no one in particular, as he grabbed his jacket. "I'll go."

His hand had just touched the door knob, when Dr. Paul called out, "Jamie." in the middle of a wide yawn.

Shoot! "Sir?" Jamie paused but didn't turn to look at the man, afraid he might be in trouble again. Did he know Melinda had fallen trying to get out of bed? What had she told him ? Did he know it was all Jamie's fault, because he hadn't stayed awake? He looked down at his hands, which gripped his jacket so hard, they'd turned white.

"Melinda tells me you stayed and helped keep her calm while Robbie was gone."

Jamie's immediate relief evaporated, overtaken by a deep embarrassment; he shrugged in a self-deprecating manner.

"You did a good job keeping her mind occupied and making her comfortable," the doctor persisted.

Not knowing how to react to this unexpected praise, Jamie finally mumbled, "I didn't do much. Just sat there, mostly."

"Sometimes, the most important thing you can do for a patient is to sit with them and let them know they're not alone." Dr. Paul became thoughtful, as if remembering other cases. "Sometimes, it's the only thing you can do," he added softly.

The memory of his mother's bedside came to mind. Jamie pictured both his father and the doctor sitting with her through the night, speaking in low murmurs, occasionally wiping her face with cool cloths. Was that what the man was talking about? In his conflicted mind, opposing thoughts struggled to establish the truth. His father wasn't responsible for what happened; he had no medical knowledge. But Dr.

Paul did, and still he'd just sat on his hands. He was just making excuses for letting Ma die! Jamie was certain of it. But then he thought, *What if it's true? What if sometimes that really is all you can do?* He shook his head in confusion, and then, the dam burst.

"You're just making that all up! My ma didn't have to die!" he hissed, so angry he could barely speak the words. "You just sat there and did nothing. You could've saved her, but you didn't!" His voice rose. "You let her die!" he shouted. "You killed her!"

Like a runner at the end of an exhausting race, he couldn't catch his breath; his entire body shook so violently he was afraid he might fall over. Leaning forward, he grabbed the back of a chair for support.

"Jamie, no!" "Stop this, son." Robbie and his father were both shouting, shocked by his vitriol.

Dr. Paul remained calm. When he spoke, his voice was weary, but soft, "Let it all go, Jamie. Let it all go."

Finally emptied of all the angry words he'd been storing up for so long, Jamie stood silent.

In the same patient tone, the doctor continued, "I tried everything I could to make your mother comfortable, to ease her pain. But I knew from the first she wasn't likely to make it. She was too ill by the time I arrived. But with pneumonia, even if I had been called at the start, there's no guarantee I could have saved her."

Turning away, he looked towards the window for a moment, and Jamie was struck by the deep anguish on the man's face. Still, he couldn't resist another shot. "I don't believe you," he hissed.

Dr. Paul turned back and looked into his eyes, "Jamie, I'm going to tell you something few people know. Medicine is more of an art than a science."

"What's that supposed to mean?" His breath was returning in gasps. "Some kind of riddle? It's just more fancy words! You're a fake. You're not a doctor. You're a murderer!"

"Jamie!" Robbie's shocked voice called out. "Stop this!"

"No, it's not a riddle," the doctor continued, ignoring Robbie. "It's an ancient truth. It means sometimes the 'art' of medicine is all we have, when the science of it fails. The art is in sitting with the patient through the crisis and hoping and praying they survive. Because, when we've run out of treatment options, sometimes, that's all there's left to do. You sit with the patient and pray for the best." He slumped back in his chair, brushing a strand of hair out of his eyes, and looking exhausted. His eyes closed. Silence filled the small space. None of the MacGregors spoke.

When his eyes reopened bare seconds later, he added, "Sadly, it doesn't always work. It didn't with your mother. I sincerely wish it had. As a doctor, there is nothing worse than losing a patient, especially as fine a person as Sarah was, but I did everything I could to save her, believe me. Everything. I think your father understands." Joseph Paul's gray eyes studied Jamie's contorted face. "And I believe your mother did, too. I hope one day you will."

"It's all talk! Words! You don't know anything," Jamie cried. He was tired. Tired of everything. To his horror, his eyes filled with tears. No! He couldn't cry!

"And isn't that what you did with Melinda this afternoon?" the doctor suggested. "Think about it: you sat with her, held her hand, talked to her, and kept her comfortable, because that was all you could do. You've no idea how much that meant to her."

Jamie slumped into the chair, no longer able to summon any anger. He was so very tired.

Robbie placed a mug of tea before the doctor, who took a long, grateful sip and thanked him, before turning to Jamie again. "And that was also an excellent idea you had to raise her feet on those blankets. She says it helped."

Jamie was aware of his father and brother regarding him with entirely different expressions, almost as if they were pleased.

"What made you think of that?" Dr. Paul asked.

Jamie really didn't want to engage in this conversation any longer, but his brother and father looked so eager to hear.

"I don't know. It just came to me." He glanced at his father. "I used to see Ma do it sometimes. I thought it might help." His father's face broke into a wide grin.

"Well, it did." When Dr. Paul actually reached out and put a hand on his shoulder, Jamie's entire body stiffened, wondering what was coming next. He was not prepared for the words that followed.

"Good man!"

Grateful for the distraction of the mug Robbie handed him, Jamie held it to his nose, breathing in the warm, fragrant steam from the hot tea. It helped to clear his spinning head and clouded thinking. Nothing more was said, and as the doctor set out for home, Jamie finally succumbed to sleep with those two words repeating in his mind, 'good man.'

*****

When morning broke, Jamie and his da held a whispered conversation. Robbie had gone home the night before to tend to the animals but would soon return for Melinda, who remained asleep.

For Jamie, the familiar sense that he was a disappointment to his father had been replaced by the exhilarating knowledge that with yesterday's actions, he'd made him proud.

"Well, that was quite a day," Da said. "Not one I'd care to see again. No, sir. But all's well that ends well, eh, lad?"

"Guess so."

"You guess so? For goodness sake! Your brother's very grateful for how you handled things. Aye, and so am I." More quietly, he added, "Your Ma would be proud, too."

Jamie couldn't believe what he was hearing. He thought if he never lived another day, he'd die happy.

Chapter Thirty-One

New Life and A Death

Spring had officially arrived weeks ago, but it didn't feel like it. Now, it announced its true arrival with a flourish. The last stubborn mounds of snow in the bush disappeared within two or three days, and clusters of fresh-faced white trilliums replaced them. In some spots, the blooms were so thick, a person might imagine a few of those little patches of snow still remained.

The sudden melt resulted in gurgling streams pushing their way through earthy cracks and crevices and over and around rocks, seeking the path of least resistance to continue on their way to lakes and rivers. Roads, formerly frozen hard in winter, thawed into soft, muddy traps for travellers.

*****

Something new was afoot in Jamie's world. Melinda flourished in her pregnancy, looking healthy and happy at last. There were no more scares, for which all were grateful. Robbie and Da, although not given to emotional speeches, continued to let Jamie know how appreciative they were that he'd overcome his own fears and acted with such maturity on that frightening day. To everyone's relief, Da's shame over being too drunk to help in that crisis brought an immediate change.

Melinda herself seemed to have assumed the role of big sister, sometimes fussing over Jamie, and at other times embarrassing him with her teasing . She loved to go on about how precious he must have looked in that fancy Christening gown he'd found in his mother's dresser drawers. "What an adorable baby you must have been," she'd say." Especially in that bonnet, all tied up in ribbons." Then she'd pinch his cheeks for good measure, and laugh when he'd turn red and protest. He knew her teasing was all good-natured, and, deep down, it pleased him, because his most fervent wish was coming true. The MacGregors were forming a real family again, comfortable with each other and eagerly awaiting the arrival of a new member.

On Saturdays, Jamie eagerly anticipated his time in the store. He enjoyed the customers' comings and goings on this busiest day of the week and helping them with their orders, when he could.

Many people stopped to gossip, and he learned all the latest, but he also learned useful things. When it came to something he didn't know, or didn't know how to do, he only had to ask, and someone would have the answer. This was a community of pioneers, after all, and in order to survive, people had learned how to be self-sufficient in many ways, from growing their own food, to hunting for it. To these people in particular, a trip to town was a life-line to their community. Many had moved from densely-populated towns and cities and now felt isolated, living in the bush where they rarely saw a neighbour.

The landscape was changing, too, with the arrival of a few new families clearing their allotted parcels of land for farming.

In addition to the new blacksmith shop, someone had donated a plot of land further down the street for a church and the men of the community were erecting a simple building. Progress was slow, as work was done in their spare time, of which there was very little. Four walls and a bare roof stood awaiting windows and shingles before rain, and eventually snow, could do damage.

Church-goers sat on rough benches made from felled trees during Sunday services, which they took turns leading while waiting for a minister to answer their call. With luck, a circuit-riding preacher would add them to his rounds. They would be one of several villages he'd serve.

At the opposite end of town, another building was being built partly from timber and partly from stones removed from nearby fields. Square and squat, it had a practical look to suit a practical purpose. This would be a town hall and, if and when necessary, a jail.

Along with the arrival of new families and the erecting of new buildings, came the annual infestation of blackflies and then mosquitoes. It seemed no sooner were people enjoying the pleasure of being outdoors again after a harsh winter, than nature decided to spoil their fun by sending these pests.

Even animals suffered. Deer and moose fled the safety of the bush, seeking relief from the biting insects. This led to more than a few dangerous situations when a moose, driven mad by the flies, encountered an unsuspecting traveler on the road, or a farmer in his field. However, with luck, the result of these confrontations was often a bit of welcome meat, as by this time of year, most families were coming to the end of the winter provisions they'd set aside the previous fall.

In mid-May, Mr. Boyle passed away. His death was not unexpected, as he'd been unwell for several months, but still the village mourned the loss of a kind man and one of its early citizens. The store remained closed for three days, its doors and windows draped in black cloth. At his funeral, held in the new, unfinished church, many told stories of the man's kindness. He had often helped others in a quiet, private manner, expecting nothing in return.

Dr. Paul expressed his concern about Mrs. Boyle's well-being to his wife, "We all became so used to hearing their frequent bickering with each other in the store, we missed an important point. Since they had no family at all, not even siblings, the two of them were especially close."

What he didn't say was Mrs. Boyle had decided she had nothing and no-one to live for anymore, and he was unable to persuade her otherwise. As her doctor, as well as her friend, his inability to help her frustrated him. He knew if she continued in this frame of mind, she wouldn't be long for this world either.

Chapter Thirty-Two

The Worm Turns

On a fine Saturday morning in June, the first thing Jamie did on arriving at the store was remove the black mourning cloths draped across the windows. Although he respected the custom, their presence had been oppressive, and he was glad to see them go.

He and Andrew would continue to wear their black armbands out of respect for Mrs. Boyle, who remained in mourning, secluded in her rooms above the store. The only visitors she permitted were Andrew and the doctor. Jamie felt for her loss. Still he couldn't help enjoying the newly lightened mood in the store.

"Well, that job's done," Jamie called out to Andrew some time later, after packing the drapes in boxes and putting them in storage. "Mind if I take a short break?" Without waiting for an answer, he headed for the back door.

*****

Closing his eyes, Jamie enjoyed the warmth of the sun on his face. Here on the back steps of the store, he could stretch out his legs, lean back on his elbows, and savour the moment. He tried to remember the last time he'd felt like this: almost…happy. Certainly not in the months since his mas died. He was reluctant to even use that word now, just in case "the gods" were listening. He used to make fun of his mother's tales about the wee folk, the fairies. But now, he acknowledged a primal fear that if he said he was happy, something terrible would happen. However, he did allow himself one heck of a big, self-satisfied smile, and it felt great.

"You like this job?" The question startled him. Carr! Damn! He should have known better than to let his guard down. He sighed, knowing his quiet break had come to an unwelcome end.

"What do you care?"

Carr settled himself on the step above him. "You're right. I don't."

Jamie hadn't seen anything of the disagreeable jerk for some time, and that was fine with him. At first, he'd found him intriguing, even fun, in a dangerous sort of way, but it hadn't taken long for his appeal to wear off. Life at home was now more bearable, and, yes, he did like his job. More trouble was the last thing he needed.

Making a great show of gathering up his things, he said, "Sorry. I have to get back to work."

"Nah. Yer just tryin' to avoid me. Been doin' that for a while now."

"No, I haven't. I've just been busy. Besides, I haven't seen you around much. Where've you been hiding?" He couldn't care less where Carr had been. He'd just thrown out the question as a diversion, not expecting an answer.

"None o' your damned business where I been," Carr exploded. "I don't report to you!"

"All right! I don't give a damn anyway. I just said...Oh, forget it."

Now that he was on his feet, Jamie noticed a change in Carr's appearance. In fact, he looked almost presentable: his formerly matted, oily hair appeared washed and trimmed, and his work clothes were not quite as foul-smelling as in the past. Even his face looked reasonably clean of grease. Jamie wondered what lay behind this. Was it to please Mr. Carr? He couldn't imagine the burly smithy cared.

Carr stood up and faced him. "Why so unfriendly, anyways? Thought we was pals."

"You're joking, right? All you've done is try to get me in trouble."

"Me?" Carr tried to look insulted. "Nah," he said, shaking his head. "I'd say ya done a pretty good job o' that all by yerself."

Somewhere in the back of Jamie's mind, a small alarm began to sound, but he ignored it. After all, what could Carr possibly know about anything? "What's that supposed to mean?"

"Ya sure caused a lot o' excitement wavin' that pistol around at the doc's. How'd ya get that thing, anyway? Steal it?"

So that was it. Relief swept over him. Almost everybody around owned a shotgun, but pistols were much more rare. Naturally, Carr would want to know all about it.

"Course I didn't steal it. It belongs to the doc. He misplaced it, and I found it, that's all. He's got a whole collection of them."

"Does he, now?" Carr's eyes lit up.

Fool! Jamie could have kicked himself for mentioning the collection.

Carr spat on the ground. "Anyways, that's not the way I heard it."

"Well, you heard wrong. Why would I steal an old piece of junk that doesn't even work." He was dying to know the source of the story. Surely not Caleb? It was against his better judgement, but the question bothered him too much not to ask. "Who told you about it, anyway?"

"Wouldn't you like to know? I keep my eyes open, ya know, and see a lot o' very interesting things." This was accompanied by a truly evil smile. "More 'n people realize, Jamie m' boy."

Waiting for what was coming next, Jamie began chewing on a fingernail to soothe his nerves.

"That's why I've been away, planning a new idea," Carr said, as he poked Jamie in the ribs. "This one will get us everything we ever wanted. I thought you might be interested, especially hearing you can get your hands on some guns. Oh, it's gonna be big."

The small alarm in the back of Jamie's mind now burst into a torrent of clanging bells. "You're crazy. There's no way in hell I want any part of that," he spat out, as he started up the steps. "Besides, I already have everything I want."

Carr blocked his way for a moment, just long enough to hiss, "You might regret that."

Jamie sucked in his breath. Did Carr have something else on him, something worse?

Chapter Thirty-Three

Francis

As soon as he entered the store, Jamie slammed the door behind him, paused, and forced himself to exhale. Ever since he started working in this store, he'd come to love its ordered environment of shelves and supplies, and its familiar smells of wood, and smoke, and burlap sacks. This place had become a rare oasis, especially when his life was in turmoil. Like he'd told Carr, he did have what he wanted —at least most of it. Except it was all in jeopardy now, including this job, if that rat really did have something over him —but what could it be?

After all, he hadn't actually stolen a pie, and that attempt to cut the harness hadn't really worked. Anything else he could think of was so minor…unless…no, he couldn't possibly know the worst…could he?

Andrew broke into his thoughts, "Hey, lazybones, rest time's over."

Embarrassed, Jamie took his place behind the counter. "Sorry. I'm on it." No sooner had he spoken than Samantha entered the store with her mother, who greeted him with a kind smile. "Good morning. It's Jamie, isn't it?"

Almost overcome with nervousness, he struggled to respond. "Yes, Ma'am."

"Hi, Jamie." Samantha stood behind her mother, a cheerful smile on her face.

Now, he blushed with shame. First her mother was nice to him, and now Samantha was grinning at him. How could they? After what he had done to their family? Flustered, his only choice was to act all business with them.

"Can I help you with something, Ma'am?"

"We're going to look at some fabric, thank you. Samantha needs a new dress." Gazing with pride at her daughter, she added, "She's grown so tall this winter – such a young lady now." It was Samantha's turn to blush, as her mother beamed at her.

"Yes, Ma'am," was all Jamie could manage.

"If I can get a start on it today, I could have it done in time for the Confederation Day celebrations. July 1st isn't too far off."

"Yes, Ma'am." Jamie didn't know what else to say.

"Will you and your father be coming into town for the festivities?"

"I—I don't know, Ma'am," Jamie stumbled over the words. "We don't usually go to parties."

"Oh, you must this year. There are going to be special fireworks! I haven't seen fireworks in ages!" Mrs. Paul's excitement was contagious.

"I've never seen them before," Samantha spoke up. "You should come and watch them with us. Our veranda will be the perfect spot. We're going to make ice cream, too, for a special treat."

Jamie had never seen fireworks, either, and he'd certainly never tasted ice cream. It all sounded exciting, but

he was sure his father wouldn't want to come to town for any of it, so he didn't say anything.

"Will you come?" Samantha pressed on.

Her eagerness thrilled but also embarrassed him. So, when Mrs. Paul changed the subject, he was relieved.

"My husband tells me you were a real help during your sister-in-law's recent emergency."

"I guess so," Jamie mumbled, astonished Dr. Paul had even mentioned it.

"Now, don't be shy. You apparently handled the situation very well." Mrs. Paul smiled again before she and Samantha moved off to examine some bolts of cloth on the shelves.

Jamie was flabbergasted to hear Dr. Paul had praised him, given their history. All of a sudden, he understood why Mrs. Paul and Samantha were being so nice – they didn't know what he'd done! The doctor hadn't revealed his secret! The only one he'd confided in was Caleb.

And that meant no one else likely knew, either. The realization made him dizzy. He'd always assumed people were gossiping behind his back about the horrible things he'd done, especially after that fight on the doctor's front lawn.

Now, he no longer had to hang his head in shame; he could stand tall.

Lost in these amazing thoughts, he hadn't noticed the return of an unwanted presence.

"Well, look at the lovestruck puppy!"

Carr again! How long had he been hovering there? Determined not to react to the taunt, Jamie asked, "Can I help you?"

"Yeah, if you're not too busy moonin' over Samantha. I need nails."

This was an odd request for a blacksmith to make. Couldn't he make his own? What was Carr up to? Suspicious, Jamie struggled to keep his head. "I'll show you." He started to come out from behind the counter but was met with a raised hand in front of his face.

"Just point the way. I'll pick 'em out myself."

"Whatever you want." Jamie decided to let the unpleasant fellow have his way. He pointed to a corner. "Help yourself."

"Oh, I definitely will." But instead of heading for the barrels, Carr turned in the opposite direction.

"Good morning, Mrs. Paul," he said in a voice so sweet, Jamie couldn't believe his ears.

"Oh, good morning, Francis," Mrs. Paul smiled.

*****

So it's Francis, is it? Jamie had wondered about Carr's first name but had never been able to get one out of him. He figured the fellow must be embarrassed about it. He chuckled as Mrs. Lawson continued, "I'm just fine, thank you. And how are you?"

"Fine, thank you, Ma'am. I just came in to look for some nails," he said as if needing to explain his presence. But his real intentions soon became clear, as he turned to Samantha.

"Good morning, Samantha. You look very pretty today."

Samantha blushed. "Thank you," she replied, then turned to her mother, as if needing rescue. "I like this colour, Mother," she said, pointing to a bolt of robin's egg blue cloth.

Jamie almost felt sorry for Carr. He looked so pathetic in his obvious attempt to talk to Samantha. But was this really to do with an interest in Samantha, or was it just another taunt aimed at him?

After hanging around for a few minutes, Carr perhaps sensed Samantha's discomfort with his presence, said, "Well, I hope to see you both again soon." in a cheerful tone. "Perhaps at the big celebration."

"Yes, perhaps," Mrs. Paul replied, almost absent-mindedly. Samantha kept her head down, examining the blue fabric.

Heading for the door, he passed the counter without even looking at Jamie, who, despite his better instincts, couldn't resist saying, "Goodbye, *Francis*!"

Carr swirled around and, in a low voice snarled, "It's *Frank* to you, MacGregor! And don't forget it!"

Jamie let him go without further comment, but just moments later, the fellow stood at the window, signaling him to come out. Now what?

Outside the store, Carr greeted him with an ugly smile. "Samantha's a keeper, but I think she likes you more'n me — for now."

Jamie felt lightheaded. "What are you getting at?"

Almost gloating now, Carr spit it out, "Been out with your slingshot lately?"

A strange, gurgling sound caught Jamie's attention, and he actually looked around to determine where it was coming from, before realizing it was his own churning stomach. Carr knew!

Without saying another word, he banged through the door and rushed to the back of the store, Carr's laughter ringing in his ears. The lowlife creep not only knew, he was threatening blackmail! And not for the first time. But why? It could only be to trap him into that scary new scheme he'd been talking about, the one that required a gun. And his only way out would be to give up Samantha. Trapped! He was utterly trapped.

Breaking into his thoughts, Andrew called from the front of the store, "You all right back there?"

If there was one thing Jamie didn't need right now, it was for Andrew to find out what Carr was up to. He'd lose his job for sure. Fighting to appear normal, he made his way forward and replied, "I'm fine. It's just that idiot Carr showed up again."

"I thought maybe you and him were becomin' pals.

"No way! He's crazy."

"Well, you know I don't trust him. Just be careful— I hate to see a friend get hurt."

If you only knew, Jamie thought. The beautiful sunny day he'd been enjoying just a short time ago had turned dark. And that fear of impending disaster had shifted. It was no longer a case of if it would strike, but when. Or so it seemed.

Chapter Thirty-Four

Brotherly Advice

The next day, Sunday, Jamie walked over to Rob and Melinda's place. The day was sunny but his buzzing thoughts were almost as annoying as the swarm of blackflies endlessly attacking him. Twirling the leafy branches of a switch kept the insects at bay. It was an effective method, but it only worked on the pests. His whirling thoughts needed another kind of help, which he could only get from his brother.

When the cabin came into view, his determination faltered. But the thought of Carr's sneering face hovering around Samantha drove him onward.

Robbie met him at the door, urging Jamie to hurry inside. "Quick! Don't bring all those pests in with you. And speaking of little pests, what brings you by?" Seeing Jamie's eyes begin to flash, he became contrite. "Calm down. It's just a joke."

The delicious aroma of baking pies filled the cabin. Melinda, covered in flour, gave Robbie a playful swat and greeted Jamie with a smile. "Don't listen to Robbie. You know we're both glad to see you." She peered more closely at him. "Is everything all right?"

Everything wasn't all right, and Melinda appeared to understand. "It seems to me you might be in need of a brother-to-brother talk," she said. "I'll go in the other room. I've got plenty of knitting to catch up on."

"No need for that," Robbie said. "I think Jamie and I need to go check on the pigs."

"Well, all right, but no more teasing!" she warned.

Jamie was grateful to his brother for suggesting the barn. They'd have more privacy there.

*****

Now Jamie paced round and round the barn, a bundle of anxiety,

"So, is it Da?" Robbie's eyes followed him around the small space.

"No, Da's been good lately."

"Well, thank goodness for that. Must make it easier for you." Rob snatched a straw from the bale and began chewing on it.

"Yeah, that's true. It's just…"

"Just what? Don't keep me in suspense. Out with it."

Jamie hesitated. He peered in at the noisy pigs and watched the little ones suckling. They looked cozy and peaceful. He'd like to feel peaceful, too, but that meant getting through this hard conversation first.

Realizing there was no other way out— a feeling confirmed by his brother's intent gaze— Jamie took a deep breath and let the whole sad tale spill out.

While Jam talked, Robbie listened carefully.

"Listen, little brother," he broke in, "That's one heck of a mess you've gotten into—way more 'n anythin' I ever managed, and I managed to get into quite a few."

"I remember, but that doesn't help me now."

"I guess. But I always got out of it, and you will too. You'll have to face it—not just Carr, but Samantha, as well. She'll have to be told."

Jamie groaned as his brother continued. "It's not gonna be easy, but I know you can do it."

For a while, the only sound was of the pigs rooting around in their straw and muck. Even Blackie was unusually quiet in her stall.

"All right, I'll do it."

"When?" Robbie pressed.

"Tomorrow." It felt good to have made his decision. "Thanks, Robbie."

"Anytime. Now, come on in and have some pie. Melinda's getting pretty good at baking lately."

Chapter Thirty-Five

Face-Off

Walking home, Jamie felt so buoyed by his talk with Robbie that even the three pieces of Melinda's pie he'd gobbled couldn't weigh him down. He knew his brother was right. He could figure things out— all he had needed were some words of encouragement from someone he trusted.

Now, he was determined to find Samantha and confess to her. He could go into town tomorrow when school got out. The idea was still daunting. Maybe he should face down Carr first?

But speak of the devil, as he rounded a curve close to home, there was his nemesis straddling the road. In spite of his bravado, Jamie felt a pang.

"Now what?" he demanded, his voice sullen.

Carr replied with typical cockiness. "Don't get excited. Can't a fella just be out for a walk?"

"When did you ever just go for a walk?" Jamie grumbled. He could have pushed past the bully but, remembering Robbie's words, decided he had to try holding his ground.

Carr looked him up and down. "I thought we could have a nice little chat," he said with a nasty smirk.

"I've got nothing to say to you." Jamie tried to stand tall.

"That's not nice. I think we have lots of things to talk about, especially things I know about you..."

With growing impatience, Jamie shot back, "Oh really, *Francis*? Well, you know what?"

"No, what, Jamie-boy? Is that what she calls ya? 'Jamie-Boy'?" The sneer had returned. "Or is it, 'Jamie, dear'? " The words were spoken in a high-pitched attempt to mimic a young girl. The mocking laugh that followed was bitter.

"What're you talking about?" Jamie demanded. "Who? Who's 'she'?"

"Don't act like ya don't know. I told ya I see everythin'. Samantha, o' course! You two are sweet on each other. It's so obvious, it's sickenin'." Without warning, he spat a glob of mucous in Jamie's face.

"You bugger!" Truly angry now, Jamie wiped the mess off his face, then lunged forward, knocking Carr on the dirt with a heavy thud, where he lay choking in the cloud of dust that rose around him. Snorting hard, like a young bull ready for a fight to the death, Jamie watched as the cretin pulled himself up, still gasping for breath.

Suddenly, he was struck with the thought that it was time to just put this whole thing to rest.

I'm going home," he sighed. "You can go to hell, as far as I'm concerned. You've got nothing on me, *Francis!*"

"Stop calling me that!" Carr managed to spit out. "And I got plenty on ya."

"No, you don't. Dr. Paul knows everything." Seeing his challenger's sceptical look, he decided to embellish this statement just a bit more. "So does Andrew. Lots of people know. So, you can't push me around anymore. It's over."

"You're lyin'. Why aren't ya locked up then? And how come you're workin' in the store? They wouldn't just let ya get away with it. Nah, ya can't fool me. You're lyin' all right."

"You believe what you want, but I'm telling the truth. He knows. And I'm working in the store to repay him for the window."

As soon as he said the last part, Jamie realized this was something he wanted to do. No, had to do.

"So, we're done here." He headed for home. His body ached and his head throbbed, but he was relieved he'd confronted Francis Carr, and the truth was out.

True to form, Carr claimed the last word. "Not so fast, Jamie-boy. Samantha doesn't know yet, right?" He paused to let his words sink in. "Unless I've already told her… hmmm…" His nasty laughter filled the air, as he turned and walked away.

*****

Jamie ran until he could go no further. Bile filled his mouth, and he bent over to spit it out in the mud. For an instant, he wished that mud would swallow him whole. Two warring factions had set up camp in his already throbbing head. One insisted Carr would never tell her. Of course, he would, the other side argued. He'd delight in it.

Would he do it? Had he already done it? Jamie didn't want to believe it was possible, but with Carr you never knew. All the exhilaration he'd felt earlier in the day, fizzled out like a dying fire. What was he to do? He began to dread the next time he saw the girl.

Chapter Thirty-Six

Celebration!

July 1st arrived, pleasantly warm, but without the heavy, exhausting humidity people had complained about the week before. In contrast to how sluggish and irritable many had been, the village now hummed with excitement, and everyone declared it was going to be a perfect night for the much anticipated fireworks display.

Jamie and his father had been invited, along with Andrew, to join the Pauls for dinner and later watch the fireworks from their veranda. To Jamie's relief, his father, who wasn't one for parties and fuss, had declined the invitation. "But you should go, lad," he'd insisted. "It's more for the young, anyway."

As much as he'd been tempted, especially by the thought of seeing Samantha, he still didn't know whether or not Francis Carr had exposed his secret. Nothing had been said by anyone else, and he'd been relieved not to run into her. He made excuses. "It'll be over late. I don't think I want to walk home alone then."

"For goodness sake! You'll be sure to hitch a ride with some of the neighbours. Or you could bed down in the store. Go, lad."

Wanting to put an end to the discussion, Jamie sighed, "All right. I'll think about it."

But when Caleb came into the store later that day, Jamie said he and his da couldn't come. "Please thank your mother for the invitation."

"That's too bad," Caleb replied almost absent-mindedly, and nothing more was said. This off-handed response was unexpected; Jamie would have expected more animosity. Surely Caleb would be thrilled not to have him there?

Andrew, however, had tried all kinds of persuasion throughout the week. First it was the food. "How can you pass up a delicious chicken dinner? You don't eat that well at home."

Then it was Samantha. "She'll be so disappointed. Are you sure you want to break her heart?"

He returned to the food. "Chantal says they're making ice cream! You can't say no to that!"

Finally, he pleaded for himself. "Please, Jamie, help me out here. I'm too nervous to go alone."

He believed Andrew was every bit as uptight as he was, but he wasn't sure why. Andrew hadn't done anything as dastardly as interrupting the doctor's wedding in such a terrible way. In fact, Andrew and the doctor were on quite friendly terms.

*****

Now the day was here, and in between customers, Andrew kept asking him to change his mind, but Jamie stood firm. He knew Andrew didn't understand, and he didn't want to have to explain why he was uncomfortable about accepting the invitation.

Some of Andrew's pleading made him laugh out loud, but he just kept saying, "Da's expecting me home."

Part-way through the afternoon however, Doctor Paul came into the store and approached him. "What's this I hear? Caleb says you're not coming tonight for the fireworks? Surely, that can't be true?"

Dumbstruck and confused, Jamie didn't know what to do or say. Dr. Paul had actually come looking for him. And sounding disappointed he wasn't coming.

Andrew spoke up, "I've been working on him for days to change his mind. He should come."

"Of course, he should," Dr. Paul agreed. "Jamie?"

The two waited for an answer. Jamie felt the pressure of their expectations, and he was flattered by their insistence. It was obvious they really wanted him at the party, but he felt compelled to resist.

Unable to meet their hopeful eyes, he fibbed once again, "No, I can't. Sorry. Da's expecting me home."

"I know your father turned down the invitation, but that doesn't mean you can't come. I'm sure he'll understand. Besides, you can't turn down a chicken dinner and ice cream, can you? I insist. The young people will be disappointed if you don't join us. We'll have a perfect view of the fireworks display from our front veranda."

Jamie was completely taken aback by this personal approach. Imagine Dr. Paul coming to the store to insist he come!

"Your father will likely conclude you just changed your mind and decided to stay after all. I don't think he'll worry too much."

Suddenly, both the sincere invitation and the temptation of all the fun and excitement overwhelmed him. Jamie knew his father actually wanted him to stay. He'd made that clear. He decided not to worry about what Carr might or might not have told Samantha. He was beginning to think the bully had lied once again, anyway. Of course, if he hadn't told Samantha, that meant he might be licking his wounds and biding his time to try something else. Jamie dismissed the thought. At the moment, he was too happy. The evening sounded too exciting to turn down.

"All right, " he said. "Thank you. I'll come."

Andrew slapped him on the back. "Atta boy!"

"I'm glad." Dr. Paul agreed, with a warm smile. " We'll all look forward to seeing you later."

When the door closed behind the doctor, Jamie found Andrew staring at him. "So that's what it takes, eh? A personal invitation from the doctor himself?" Andrew sniffed, and turned his back, pretending to be offended. "My invitation wasn't good enough?"

His antics brought a chuckle from Jamie, who felt the promise of an unbelievable evening ahead. "The young people will be disappointed," the doctor had said. He hoped that included Samantha.

Chapter Thirty-Seven

Heaven

On the front veranda, some settled themselves in comfortable chairs, while others lounged on the broad steps, relaxing after their delicious meal. On the back porch, Mrs. Paul and her daughters fussed with the ice-cream making. Jamie MacGregor decided he was in heaven. Or at least, this was how he thought heaven would feel. If the ice cream treat lived up to the amazing chicken dinner, it would further confirm this belief.

He wondered what was involved in the process. From what he'd heard, it sounded like something magical. Since he'd never tasted this treat before, he didn't know what to expect, except that it would be cold. Everyone else was certainly excited about it. Even if it turned out a disappointment, it wouldn't matter. He would still be in heaven. Just being with this happy group of family and friends, was unexpected but delightful, and having been placed beside Samantha at the dinner table had put him over the moon.

He'd worried about what to talk about and about his table manners and all kinds of other things, but with so many people there and mostly talking all at once, there'd been no need for him to say anything at all. Once or twice someone had asked a question of him, and he'd managed a reply. As for Samantha, she'd made it easy, smiling and chatting about everything under the sun, it seemed. At one point, in her excitement to explain something, she'd placed a hand on his arm, and he'd almost jumped out of his skin. Had she noticed? Did she feel his entire body heat up and see how red his face burned? She'd removed her hand quickly. Had she felt the same heat? These questions continued to set his brain ablaze.

As the meal progressed, he confirmed his suspicion that Francis Carr had yet to tell Samantha anything about what happened on her parents' wedding day. Surely, she wouldn't be behaving as friendly as she was if she knew? He was doubly glad he'd decided to accept the invitation,, if only to put that worry out of his mind. For the time being. He wasn't dumb enough to think Carr was finished with him yet. No, there would be more threats and devious behaviour to come, unless Jamie told Samantha himself. And he would. But not tonight. Tonight was too special to risk spoiling. Tomorrow, for sure.

He realized May Whylie was speaking to him. "I'm so excited about the fireworks. Aren't' you? " Without waiting for an answer, she raced on. "We were supposed to come much earlier. But our little calf escaped, and we had to round her up. She was so funny. I think she thought she could outsmart father, zig-zagging back and forth, but he caught her."

Her father scowled. "'t weren't funny!"

"Now, Jim, " Mrs. Whylie interrupted. "Don't carry on so." She turned to Dr. Paul, who had just come out and settled into a chair. "I just hope things go well, tonight. Mr. Zammatt came by as Jim was hitchin' the horses up. He says there's a whole box of those fireworks missin'. He sure was all worked up about it."

"Probably just forgot where he put 'em," Jim Whylie huffed. "Knucklehead!"

"I don't think so. He thinks they've been stolen, but why would anybody do that? You can't use them for anythin' else."

"Jim's likely right," Dr. Paul said. "Mr. Zammatt has probably just mislaid them."

"Well, at least there'll still be some fireworks. I'm so glad we could come," May said, turning to Jamie. "Samantha says Chantal won't let anyone talk about the ice cream they've made. She wants it to be a big secret."

"Too late for that. Everyone seems to know," Jamie commented.

"I know, but just for fun, let's pretend we don't. Chantal loves having secrets. She just can't keep them very well."

"And that's a fact," Caleb put in. "Don't ever trust Chantal with your deepest secret. Not even a little unimportant one. Nothing's safe with her." He was laughing as he said this. Jamie had observed that Caleb adored all his sisters, but he had an especially soft spot for Chantal.

Samantha appeared at the door. "The ice cream is ready. And the fireworks will start soon." She gave Jamie a special smile. "I think you're going to love the ice cream."

Caleb had missed the ice cream announcement. His attention had been drawn to something else. Pointing to a figure rushing past, he said, "There's a fellow always about somethin', and it's usually not good." With a sarcastic laugh, he added, "Idiot! He's even goin' in the wrong direction, if he plans on seeing the fireworks."

At that moment, the figure looked up. Francis Carr! Jamie recoiled, not wanting to be seen with Samantha at that moment, but it was too late.

"It figures!" Carr stopped to shout. "Enjoy it while you can, Jamie, me boy. She won't want any part of ya when she knows the truth!"

Samantha gasped, looking stricken. Jamie wished he could disappear through the floor, but instinctively, he put a hand out to her, and she took it.

"You shut up, Carr!" Caleb shot back. "You're not welcome here!"

"Pretty soon, Jamie-boy won't be, either." With that, the bully rushed off, looking pleased.

An embarrassed silence enveloped the porch. Jamie dropped Samantha's hand. She looked at him, puzzled. "What did he mean?" she asked.

Jamie couldn't answer, nor could he bear to look at anyone else.

Andrew had also observed Carr. He walked over to Caleb and Jamie. "What do you think? Should we go after the troublemaker?"

"Nah. I don't like the guy, and he's got no business spoutin' off like that," Caleb replied. "But there's no point goin' after him. It wouldn't make any difference."

Jamie didn't want to go after Carr, tonight of all nights, so he didn't reply to Andrew's question.

"Hey, Samantha!" Carr's faint voice reached their ears from a distance, "Guess you're not as smart as you think you are, fallin' for him!"

There were shocked gasps from those close enough to have heard.

"That's it!" Caleb shouted, heading down the steps. "You comin'?" he called back to Andrew

"You bet! "Andrew was on his heels. "Comin', Jamie?"

Jamie didn't reply. He'd caught a look of doubt in Caleb's eyes. Samantha's brother still didn't trust him completely. Andrew caught the look, too. "He'll be fine," he assured Caleb. "We can trust him."

"Be careful," warned Mr. Whylie, who was one of those who had overheard Carr's insult.

Thankfully, Samantha was one who hadn't. While confused as to why the three were suddenly taking off, she nevertheless called after them, " Hurry back. We'll save some ice-cream for you!"

Chapter Thirty-Eight

A Night to Remember

Francis Carr and the three boys weren't the only ones on the move. This was the biggest event the village had ever held, and everyone wanted to be part of it. Large groups of people soon filled the open space along the river bank, where the fireworks display would take place. Most in the crowd were villagers, but others had walked in from nearby farms. A wagon loaded with two or three families drew up, and a troop of excited children tumbled out. Blankets dotted the ground, and a festive bonfire blazed. To add to the excitement, a pack of local dogs ran in frantic circles, barking at everyone. It was quickly becoming impossible to move.

"There he is!" Andrew nudged Jamie's shoulder and pointed to Carr standing at the back of the crowd.

"Keep going!" Caleb said.

Pushing and shoving their way through the throng, they made frustratingly little headway. Suddenly, Andrew pointed ahead. "He's moving! Looks like he's heading to his place."

'We'll never catch up," Caleb huffed in frustration. "Damn!"

Jamie looked around, getting his bearings. Everything looked different in the midst of a milling crowd. "I know a way," he said. "There's a path we can take behind some buildings. It'll bring us out near Carr's place."

"You sure? I don't remember anything like that," Caleb said.

"Follow me," Jamie said, leading the way behind a building, away from the noise and bustle. The path had become more of a dumping ground than he remembered, and thus created a hazard in the gathering darkness.

"Ow!" Andrew hit his shin on a discarded barrel and stopped to rub his leg.

"Are you gonna be all right?" Caleb's concern was obvious. If they ran into trouble and Andrew couldn't keep up, he'd feel responsible.

"Don't worry about me," Andrew said. "I know I'm the one that got you into this, but I can handle it. I just have to know what he's up to. I got a feelin' in my bones it's nothin' good. Especially tonight, with all this crowd here."

Caleb gasped. "You mean he could be plannin' somethin', because so many people are in town? "

"I wouldn't put it past him, " Jamie said, absent-mindedly kicking at some debris on the ground. Trying to figure out what Carr was up to frustrated him no end. He kicked again, then stooped to pick up the item and examine it. A firecracker! He turned to show it to the others, just as they all heard someone running up ahead.

"The fireworks!" Andrew whistled. "I knew he was up to something. He was acting too strange earlier. But this..." He shook his head, speechless at the boldness of the act.

"We gotta get him!" Caleb said to Jamie. "You lead the way."

*****

As the sky darkened, the mood of the crowd brightened even more. Someone picked up a fiddle and scratched out a foot-stomping jig; another joined in with a flute. The enthusiastic crowd clapped to the tune, and a couple of drunks attempted to dance, their stumbles and tumbles eliciting disapproving clucks from some and laughter from others.

Jamie, having brought the others out from the alley to a convenient spot for observing the blacksmith's shop, thought how vulnerable those celebrators would be if someone had formed a plan to cause harm. He looked at his companions, who seemed to be thinking much the same thing.

"What next?" Caleb asked.

"We get in closer to the shop," Andrew replied.

Darkness cloaked most of the blacksmith's shop, but one of the two large doors stood slightly open, revealing a faint glow from the dying embers in the forge. Mr. Carr moved into view, but there was no sign of Francis.

"Let's get around the other side of the shop," Jamie suggested. "Near the stables."

"Then what?" Caleb asked.
"We'll figure it out when we get there. Let's go."

No sooner had they made it to the far side of the structure than angry voices rose from inside. Jamie stiffened and exchanged anxious glances with Andrew and Caleb. Had they been seen?

The shouted words were indistinguishable, but whatever was going on between father and son, the fight came to an end with the sound of running footsteps heading towards the back of the building. Slipping around to the rear corner, Caleb, Andrew, and Jamie observed Francis Carr charge across the yard and disappear inside the stables. Tense moments passed as they waited for whatever would come next, then Carr reappeared and took off.

"What do you make of all that?" Caleb asked.

"Well, for one thing, I'd hate to be Carr, with that father," Andrew commented. "And for another, I think we ought to check out the stable. If he's got that box of fireworks, he could have them stashed there."

"Didn't look like he was carryin' anythin'," Caleb said. "But it's getting' too dark to see much. You're right, we better have a look. Ready?" He stood up.

Jamie put a hand out to stop him. "First, we'd better make sure his old man isn't going to come out looking for him and find us instead."

"Good thinking," Caleb agreed, stepping back. "Maybe he'll go to bed soon, and then we'll have our chance. Long as Francis doesn't come back first."

As they sat back and waited for the lights to go out in the living quarters behind the shop, every minute crept by in an agony of tension, but finally all was in darkness.

A quick glance into the stables revealed two horses, both asleep on their feet.

"I can have a quick look 'round here," Jamie whispered. "If you two keep watch."

"I'm coming with you, " Caleb insisted. "Andrew can keep watch, all right?"

It was agreed. They slipped inside and stood still beside the first horse, who opened its eyes to observe them and shook its head. Jamie gently rubbed and patted its face to calm it, glad it was a sweet old mare.

The second one pricked up its ears, alert to their presence. As Caleb moved toward it, a random explosion occurred, and the crowd by the river cheered. Both horses thrashed about, mad with fear. Whinnying and kicking at the boards penning them in, they tried to break free. It wouldn't take long before the bigger one succeeded.

Chapter Thirty-Nine

Night, Night

Andrew's warning whistle drew Caleb and Jamie's attention. Realizing they had to get out of the stables, they made a dash for it across the yard, keeping low to the ground. and met up with him.

"The old man's up again," he said. "I saw his lamp turn on, then I think he went back into the shop. What happened in there?" he asked, nodding towards the stables.

"We didn't have time for a good look" Jamie said, "And the horses are too spooked to go back. We have to get into their rooms."

"Are you crazy?" Caleb looked at Jamie as if he'd never seen him before. " We'll get caught for sure."

Whiz! Boom! Whiz! Bang! The next round of fireworks exploded into the air. They couldn't see them, but the smell of smoke drifted their way, and once again the sound of the gathered on-lookers whistling, clapping, and cheering.

Andrew said, "If he's got that box of fireworks, he's dangerous. We haven't got any choice. I'll keep watch again. But you've got to be damn fast. Carr could come back at any moment."

Reluctantly, Caleb agreed to the plan. Dropping to their knees, he and Jamie moved along the back wall until they found the back entrance. As anticipated, it was unlocked. Jamie put his ear to the wall and listened.

When the noise of the crowd died down, he heard voices in the front of the building. He had no idea what they were saying, but it sounded like there might be two people speaking. A customer? Highly unlikely. Had Francis Carr returned unseen? If he was out there with his father, that would mean no one was in the back...for now. Praying he was right, he whispered this information to Caleb, and giving him the go-ahead, watched him open the door and slip inside, before following.

They found themselves in a kind of store-room full of tools. Several worn and smelly old boots lay on the floor, and Jamie could make out the shapes of two broken chairs with jackets tossed across them. Another door lay ahead. They moved towards it and pushed gently. A slight creak brought them to a stop, and Caleb put his finger to his lips. They listened. Jamie doubted he would hear anything above his thudding heart, but the voices from the front still carried through.

The door opened without any further squeaks, but still Caleb peaked around it before entering a bedroom, where a jumbled mess of blankets and clothing littered the floor. Picking his way through them, he almost stepped on a marmalade cat, snuggled under one of the blankets. It snarled at him and took off, escaping through the open door behind him. As it brushed past Jamie, he tensed up and waited. No one came.

When he could breathe again, Jamie looked at Caleb and the two almost laughed, through sheer nerves at the ridiculousness of their situation.

Without warning, Mr. Carr's voice boomed, and they jumped.

"So you went anyway!" the smithy yelled. "I told you not to, and you went against my orders!" The sound of a mighty slap reverberated through the walls.

"Ow!" Francis Carr cried out. "I just wanted to have some fun. Everyone else is there."

"You're completely useless," his father screamed. Another slap found its mark.

A loud sob followed by running footsteps warned Jamie and Caleb: Francis Carr was headed for the back of the shop!

Caleb looked at Jamie in panic. They scanned the room for a hiding place and dove under a bed, just as Carr entered the room.

His footsteps approached the bed. Jamie held his breath. If Francis lay down, they'd be trapped there all night. He could just make out Caleb's face and figured he was thinking the same thing. The feet took a few steps away, there was the sound of a cupboard door opening, and then something heavy landed on the bed, as if thrown down hard. "Shit!" Carr's voice was furious.

Caleb and Jamie looked at each other, squeezed under the low bed, and tried communicating with their eyes. Should they take a chance and jump out? If they took Carr by surprise, they might get a head start at high-tailing it out of there before he could catch up to them. Should they wait it out? He might leave. It was unlikely he'd go back out front and face his father again, but maybe he'd take off out the back like he had earlier. Jamie thought that's what he'd do, if he were in Carr's situation.

The marmalade cat came back and slipped under the bed. Caleb sneezed and all hell broke loose.

"What the...?" Carr exclaimed.

Caleb grabbed the cat by the tail and tossed him out from under the bed. Carr jumped out of its way. Jamie moved fast, sliding out to face Carr.

"You!" was all the stunned thief could say. Then he ran straight at Jamie, and they fell to the floor in a fierce struggle.

Chapter Forty

Tying Up Loose Ends

Caleb sneezed again, as he wiggled out from under the bed. At first, he wasn't certain what to do. Run for help? Jump into the fight? Jamie seemed to be handling that all right. He looked at the bed and saw what Carr had tossed there. A long, narrow box marked, "Danger. Explosives."

"Gotcha!" he whispered triumphantly, not wanting to attract Mr. Carr's attention by shouting. As it was, the fight might bring him in any moment.

Grabbing Carr by his shirt, he half-pulled him off Jamie, while holding the valuable box at arm's length. Astonished, Carr growled like an angry animal and made a grab for it, but by then, Jamie was on his feet and got him in a bear hold.

"Sh-h-h!" Caleb warned him. "You don't want your father in here, do you?"

The fear on the fellow's face almost made Caleb feel sorry for him.

"Good boy. Now, you're going to tell us what were you planning to do with these? You weren't just keeping them for fun. You had something in mind. Was it for tonight? With everyone in town? "

"None o' your business," Carr spat out, attempting a bluff. "You got nothin' on me."

"Oh, we've got plenty." Caleb's voice was low but menacing. "And we're more than happy to hand you over to the authorities. So, why waste time? Let's just go." He grabbed a piece of rope off the untidy floor and tied Carr's hands together. Jamie maintained his bear hug all the same.

Carr, realizing they were serious, pleaded with Jamie, "Look, we've been pals. If I explain, will ya let me go?"

"We're not pals, and we never were!" Jamie hissed. But Caleb could see Jamie hesitate. Maybe seeing Carr's fear, especially of his father, was softening him a little. Or maybe Carr did have something on him, and he was weighing his options. Caleb couldn't be sure what was going through MacGregor's mind.

"Maybe we can make a deal," Jamie offered, looking to Caleb for affirmation. "Tell us, and maybe we'll let you off with a warning. But you try anything ever again, and we turn you in for sure. You have to be on your best behaviour, or the deal is off. Agreed?"

"I don't trust him one bit," Caleb said. "He'll just lie."

"I won't. Just listen, please!" Carr's haste to confess was almost pathetic. He rushed on, "Look, I stole 'em, so I could go back later and throw them into that bonfire they got goin' down there by the river. That's the truth. I swear. Now, do we have a deal?"

Caleb felt faint, imaging the consequences of such an conflagration. Jamie, white with the same fear, whispered, "Why? You could have killed people! Little children! What did anybody of them ever do to you?"

"Nothin'! That's just it. None of 'em even know I exist. But they'd sure sit up and take notice of me then, wouldn't they? Everybody would know my name! And my father— my father would have a heart attack!" He sobbed and moved to wipe away a tear, but with his hands tied, all he could manage was a swipe with his shoulder. His body shook violently.

Stunned by the outrageousness of this statement, Jamie and Caleb stood speechless.

"But I came back," Carr whispered. "I came back, 'cause I couldn't do it after all." He made another awkward swipe at his tears. "We made a deal!" he hissed, on the verge of hysteria. Still, fear of his father kept his voice low. "We made a deal. Ya gotta keep your end of it."

"Tell you what," Jamie spoke at last. "The deal was you tell us all, and we wouldn't turn you in."

Carr nodded, his eyes showing signs of hope.

"So, we'll see this box gets returned. No one knows but us, and the first time you even think of causing trouble, for anybody, we report you. Got it? " He looked to Caleb for agreement. Receiving a decidedly hesitant nod, he continued, "We're giving you a second chance, which is more than you would have given those people. You don't deserve, it, but you gotta change your ways, Carr! You gotta stop all this craziness."

"I will! I promise. Now, can you untie me?" he whispered. "You can't leave me like this."

"One more question first," Caleb said, "What did you go into the stables for? We saw you run in there, before you took off. Is there any more stuff like this in there?"

"No! I swear. I just…I was going to spend the night there, bed down in the straw. But, I couldn't stay. I had to get away, at least for a little while."

"That better be the truth," Caleb warned.

"It is. I swear." Carr kept his voice low, still terrified of being overheard. "Now, you said you'd untie me."

"I've got a better idea, " Caleb whispered back, an almost evil look on his own face. "Let's just make sure you get to bed before we leave, so you don't cause anymore trouble tonight."

Jamie looked at Caleb with the same confusion he noted on Carr's face. What was he up to? That became clear when Caleb retrieved a filthy shirt from the floor, ripped a strip off, and despite the frantic fellow's wiggling and protesting, managed to tie it around Francis' mouth. When all was secure, he nodded to Jamie, and the two lifted their trussed up quarry onto the bed and pulled a blanket over him.

"Night, night," Caleb said. "We'll see your parcel gets delivered to the proper party."

As they tip-toed out of the room, all they could see were Francis Carr's eyes, flashing with fury and fear.

"Don't worry," Caleb said to the others once they were outside. "The ropes are loose enough he can get out of them eventually. But he won't be causing any more trouble tonight."

****

"I hope we didn't miss any of that delicious ice cream," a jubilant Andrew said, as he almost ran up the steps to the Paul's veranda.

"No," Heather told him. "Lucky for you, Beatrice insisted we save some. But I'm not sure any of you deserve it, running off like that."

"When you hear the story, you'll want to make a whole fresh batch, just for the three of us," Caleb said, "And we get to choose the flavour. Right, fellas?"

"Right!" Andrew echoed, looking to Jamie for confirmation. "I think we've earned it."

"Absolutely!" Jamie declared.

*****

While Andrew and Caleb entertained the others by recounting their adventure retrieving and returning the fireworks, Jamie was content to listen and enjoy his ice cream, which greatly exceeded his expectations. The three revelled in the success of their mission and the congratulations heaped upon them.

Jamie enjoyed every minute, but at the same time, he couldn't forget the fear on Carr's face at the thought of his father's discovering what he'd done, or the hatred and humiliation when they'd tied him up.

"Well, all's well that end's well," Heather said. "But what a night! All that excitement, along with the fireworks display."

"Not to mention this ice cream," Caleb added, helping himself to more.

Samantha smiled at her brother, but Jamie noticed she seemed subdued. Perhaps all the excitement had made her tired.

Andrew's parents decided to head for home and offered Jamie a lift. He was grateful when Andrew, seeing his obvious desire to linger a little longer, suggested he could stay overnight in the store and walk home in the morning.

The Whylies and May said their goodbyes, boarded their wagon and joined several others leaving town. Jamie and Andrew remained on the veranda with the Pauls, content to watch the remaining villagers disperse on foot, some sleepy and slow, but many still in a state of high excitement and calling out goodnights.

When the time arrived to say good night, Andrew and Jamie thanked the family for an unforgettable evening. Everyone agreed it had been just that— unforgettable.

Chapter Forty-One

The Morning After

Jamie bunked down in the storeroom at the back of the store that night. Andrew left him a blanket, and after such a long, exciting day, a wave of exhaustion hit him hard. However, sleep evaded him. His mind raced back and forth all night, reviewing the past hours, from the drama of finding the missing box of fireworks to the utter joy of being with the other young people for dinner at the Pauls' house, and topping it all off later on the porch with his first ice cream.

Each of the events that had occurred in those few hours, including the great spectacle of the fireworks display reflected in the river, and being with Samantha, had affected him in a deep and meaningful way. But the one that was proving to have the most profound effect on him was what he'd overheard in the back of the blacksmith's shop. His feelings about Francis Carr bounced back and forth like a ball in a child's game of catch. But this was no game. Mr. Carr was a brute, and he was turning his son into one, too.

Footsteps sounded on stairs. Who was there? But there weren't any stairs in the cabin! His eyes flew open, and he realized sleep must have finally overtaken him after all. Through a groggy haze, the events of the previous evening returned to him, and he remembered he wasn't at home; he was in the storeroom. But then, who was going upstairs to Mrs. Boyle's rooms?

There was a knock on the door, and Andrew called in. "You awake in there? It's nine o'clock."

Nine o'clock! Jamie couldn't remember ever sleeping in that late. "I'll be right out," he called and scrambled to tidy up the blankets, as well as himself. He ran a comb through his hair and took his trousers down from the peg where he'd hung them the night before.

Today was Sunday. The store would be closed, as usual, and he'd be setting out for home as soon as he was ready.

The same footsteps were now descending the stairs as he stepped out of the storeroom, still yawning and rubbing sleep from his eyes. A solemn Dr. Paul stopped at the bottom of the narrow staircase near the front of the store.

Andrew's stricken face jolted Jamie fully awake. He looked from Andrew to Dr. Paul, uncomprehending.

Dr. Paul approached Andrew and laid a gentle hand on his shoulder. "I'm glad I decided to check on her this morning. It would have been a shock for you to find her," he said. "I'm sorry, my boy."

Tears formed in Andrew's eyes. "When?" he whispered.

"Sometime last night. She was sitting in her chair by the window, facing the river. Maybe she got out of bed for the fireworks display. When you think about it, it's rather a lovely thought, really."

"But she was alone," Andrew said. "I should have been here. I might have heard something."

"There was nothing you could have done. We all knew this was coming. And in a sense, she wasn't alone. The whole village was out there. She was watching all her friends enjoying themselves. It was a peaceful end."

"Still," Andrew said.

"We'll take care of everything," the doctor said. "I'll ask some of the women to come over and do what needs to be done."

"Can I go upstairs?" Andrew asked.

Dr. Paul hesitated. "If you want to," he said at last. "But it might be better to wait until the women have prepared her body."

Andrew nodded. "Thank you," he said and walked back to his tiny room, where he closed the door.

Dr. Paul regarded Jamie. "Well, young man…," he began.

"I'm supposed to go home shortly," Jamie said. "But maybe I should wait until the women arrive?"

"No, no. There's no need for that. But thank you for offering." He paused. "Andrew's likely going to take this very hard. The Boyles have been very good to him, you know. Especially since his accident. They gave him a job and treated him almost like a son."

Jamie nodded, "Yes, sir."

"He's going to need his friends."

"Yes, sir. I'll do what I can."

"I know you will."

Dr. Paul nodded and left the store.

Jamie followed. A friend knows when a friend needs time alone.

Chapter Forty-Two

Promises to Keep

It wasn't until a week after Mrs. Boyle's funeral that Jamie saw Francis Carr again. He stood in his usual spot, half-hidden behind the doors to his father's shop.

On an impulse, Jamie decided to wave as he passed by. It was childish he knew, but he couldn't help himself. He didn't wait for a response. He knew there wouldn't be one. Nevertheless, he couldn't resist a quick glance back over his shoulder. What he saw wasn't a scowl; instead, Carr's expression was one of uncertainty and confusion. Jamie smiled to himself and carried on his way. Not only had Carr's attempt to ruin his life by exposing his secret failed, but, thanks to Caleb's and Andrew's help, the bully had been caught with the stolen fireworks. Carr knew that, at any time, he himself could be exposed to the authorities, and his life ruined. Jamie thought, all in all, it was a fair deal, and one that was likely to hold.

A lawyer arrived one day to read Mrs. Boyle's will to a small assembled group. The childless Boyles, having come to think of Andrew as a son, had arranged to leave the general store to him. He was now the sole proprietor. Of course, one or two people displayed some jealousy at his good fortune, but most, like Jamie, were pleased for him. With luck and good management, Andrew's future looked secure, and one of the first decisions the new owner made was to hire Jamie for an extra day each week.

Life was good. Yet there remained one important thing for Jamie to do, something he dreaded.

****

She looked as pretty as ever, walking along the riverbank in her blue dress and bonnet. It was cool for July, and she tightened a shawl around her shoulders, As she did so, Jamie thought something about her had changed since he'd first seen her a few months before: she seemed more grown-up, more mature. He felt awkward and nervous in her presence.

"Hello," he said.

She turned. "Hello, Jamie." He waited for that smile, which always lifted his spirits. When it didn't appear, he tensed. Something was wrong. This wasn't the usual happy, chatty Samantha. Why did she seem so solemn? He missed her smile. Why was he so tongue-tied? Well, that one was easy. He was terrified.

He remained certain Samantha would never speak to him again once she knew his secret, because then she'd know what a truly terrible person he really was, and he was equally certain his heart would break. But the more he saw of her and her family, the more he felt like a fraud. He appreciated that Dr. Paul had kept his secret, but he felt like a liar whenever he saw Mrs. Paul and Samantha. Now, he had to confess and face the consequences. He'd made that promise to Robbie, and he knew it was the right thing to do.

But how to start? "It's lunchtime," he said, gesturing towards his small bundle and stating the obvious. "I decided to eat outside. Sun's starting to warm up a bit."

She nodded, and although she didn't speak, something about her expression made Jamie certain she had more to say.

"Want some? There's more than enough to share." *Idiot!* He chided himself for sounding like a little kid. Still she didn't speak, simply shaking her head no.

The overhead sun had worn off some of the morning's earlier coolness, but a slight breeze stirred the river and kept the worst of the mosquitoes at bay. The sound of occasional waves lapping against stones on the shoreline normally would have brought a sense of peace, but not today.

When she spoke at last, Samantha's voice sounded wistful. "Winter always seems so long, then when summer finally gets here, it goes by so fast."

Anxious to cheer her up, he said, "Yeah, but at least spring came early this year."

She nodded in agreement. "It was lovely the day of Mother's wedding."

And there it was —his opening. His opportunity to make things right.

Closing his eyes, he plunged ahead. "I remember. I was there."

She came to a halt and turned those fathomless eyes on him. Her look unnerved him, yet he managed to get the words out, "There's something I have to tell you, Samantha. Something pretty bad... "

She interrupted, her words so soft he had to strain to hear, "I know, Jamie. I know what you did."

Chapter Forty-Three

Confessions

She knew! Oh, God, she knew! He was too late. Terrified and ashamed, Jamie couldn't face Samantha. He turned away, keeping his eyes on the murky river. Certain he'd been betrayed, his voice was bitter when he asked, "How? Did your step-father tell you?"

"No. It was that awful Francis Carr. He told me."

Carr! Jamie's fury rose. The bastard had broken their deal. "When?" he demanded. "What'd he say?"

"It was a couple of days before the fireworks. He stopped me on the road and told me, bold as brass. He said he saw you put that rock through the window at Mother's wedding. I told him he was a liar, and I didn't believe him. I said he probably did it."

So, he hadn't broken the deal. It hardly mattered now when he'd told her, anyway. All that mattered was that he had told her.

Jamie's voice dropped almost to a whisper. "So, now you know it's true."

She nodded. "Francis said if I didn't believe him, go ask my step-father. He said he knew the truth."

Jamie wiped away perspiration from his forehead with the back of his hand. Despite the slight chill in the air, he felt hot. In contrast, Samantha pulled her shawl tighter.

"I'm so sorry." He couldn't look at her, afraid of seeing disappointment, even disgust. Surely, she must hate him now.

"You *should* be sorry. It was horrible, Jamie. My mother got cut by the glass. She was bleeding. Chantal was crying, and we were all scared."

"I'm sorry," he repeated, the words almost a whisper. "I mean it."

"I hope so. I was furious when I found out. Really furious."

"What did Dr. Paul tell you?"

"I didn't talk to him then, because I didn't believe Francis. I really thought he was the one who did it. Even that night of the fireworks, when he shouted those horrible things, I still didn't believe him. But the next day, I felt so confused, I asked Papa Joseph if what Francis said was true."

"And?"

"Well, first, he was just very upset with Francis for his behaviour. But I asked him again, if it was all true. Then he said yes, and what you did certainly was very wrong, especially choosing to do it at the wedding."

"He's right. That's what I wanted to tell you today. I needed to tell you, even if you hate me for it. It was a terrible thing to do."

She didn't acknowledge his statement. "Papa Joseph tried to explain to me that sometimes, especially when people lose someone very dear, they're so hurt and confused they look for someone to blame, and sometimes they act out and do things they're sorry for later. I told him that wasn't a good enough reason, and that I'd never forgive you."

"I don't blame you."

"That night," she continued, "I thought about when Pa died, and how that's exactly how I felt. Except, I blamed Caleb, because he wasn't there, and then when he came home, I was really mean to him. But it wasn't Caleb's fault how things happened. It wasn't anybody's fault. It just happened, that's all."

He paused to summon up his courage. When at last he spoke, the words came out in a whisper, "I blamed Dr. Paul when Ma died. I was so angry, I decided I had to do something. I couldn't let him get away with it. I thought no one else was going to do anything, so I did."

To Jamie's horror, tears appeared in Samantha's eyes. She blinked and turned her back to him, to hide her emotions. He longed to comfort her but didn't know what to say or do. As if acting of their own free will, his arms reached out to hug her. But the instant they touched her, he jerked and dropped his hands, as if he'd touched something blazing hot. This strange sensation of heat, and something else he didn't recognize, shot through him. Samantha's bowed head snapped up, as if she too had felt it.

Embarrassed, he said the first thing that came into his head, "So, I guess now you know, you won't want anything to do with me."

She turned back towards him but focused her gaze on the river, as if unwilling to look directly at him. "That depends. I'm really glad you were going to tell me today. And I do believe you are truly sorry. But, I need to ask you something first."

Oh, boy! She'd just given him a sliver of hope, and he didn't want to ruin that, but Jamie wondered if he was prepared for any questions this girl might ask. "Go ahead." With a silent prayer, he waited.

"This is really important, Jamie. I have to know. Do you still hate my step-father?"

"No! He could have had me charged," he pointed out. "I could have been arrested."

"He never would have done that. He's too kind."

"Besides, he's right. I guess I just needed someone to blame, too. I know now he did what he could to help Ma, just like my father said." With those few words, a massive weight lifted from his soul.

"Good!" Her hesitant smile, as she turned to him was all he needed to lift his heart.

"Does that mean we're still friends?" He need to hear the words.

"I think so." Her old smile returned, dazzling him. "Definitely!"

They turned around and began walking back to the store, side by side like friends do, but Jamie knew something had changed. Theirs was a deeper friendship now, and he wanted to jump and punch the sky.

"Wait till I see that Francis Carr!" Samantha said. "I'll tell him off. He's such a dirty tattle-tale."

Jamie sighed. "I think I'd leave Frank alone," he warned. "Everything's cleared up here now, and he has other problems."

She gave him a quizzical look. "What do you mean?"

"I can't tell you. Sorry."

"That's all right. I trust you."

And that, Jamie decided, was without question, absolutely, definitely the very best thing he had ever heard.

Chapter Forty-Four

Time to Put Away Childish Things

In late August, a period of scorching heat arrived to torture both man and beast. On one of those blistering days, in a vain attempt to cool off, Jamie moved into the shade of a tall maple beside the cabin. The oppressive, humid air offered not even a hint of a breeze to dry his perspiration. Except for a few persistent mosquitoes, nothing stirred. Not a branch, nor a leaf, nor even a blade of grass.

His father, exhausted by the heat as well as by worry over its effect on his crops, had taken refuge inside. Even the animals lay still in their pens. The relentless sun burned through a cloudless sky, and only the occasional chirp of heat bugs interrupted nature's eerie silence. As he lay on his back, Jamie thought even the smell of the grass had changed from moist and earthy to dry and dusty. Thankfully, their well hadn't dried up, as a couple of their neighbours' had. If it did, there would be tough work ahead locating another good source of water and digging for it. In the meantime, they'd have to haul water quite a distance for the animals.

Despite this myriad of busy thoughts and concerns swirling in his head, fatigue from the heat caught up to him, and his heavy eyes closed. As he drifted off to sleep, dreams of a cool and inviting place came to him, a place hidden from the sun. Even though his last visit there had been miserable, at least his cave had been cool.

Thinking of that day now brought a sense of acute embarrassment and regret. He'd been so angry. And lost. How his life had changed! Not so long ago, he'd been convinced no one cared about him. Now, he could name a long list of others who cared, starting with Da and Robbie and Melinda. And Andrew, of course. Even Dr. Paul had surprised him with the extent of his kindness and friendship.

And Samantha. Sweet Samantha! She often joined him for walks during his lunch breaks at the store, and he couldn't wait to see her each time. They seemed to be able to share their thoughts on everything under the sun, and Jamie realized just how special that was.

Rising from his spot under the maple, he brushed twigs off his pants and headed into the woods.

*****

The mosquitoes were more plentiful, but the forest hadn't yet attracted as much heat as the open space around his cabin. He made his way quickly along the familiar path and soon reached the bushes hiding the mouth of the cave. Because the entrance was so well-concealed, he'd always believed he was the only one aware of it, so he was surprised to come upon markings in the dry dirt which indicated otherwise.

He tried to comprehend what the footprints meant. Had a hunter passed by? A trapper? *Of course not; it's not trapping season*, he chided himself. Someone had been there, though. Perhaps they'd even entered his cave. Maybe they were still inside!

He hesitated. If someone was in there, they could be dangerous. A criminal, even. He shook his head and laughed, telling himself to stop imagining the worst and just go in. It was highly unlikely anyone was in there. But first, he decided, he should give some warning, just in case.

Stepping back into the bush a bit, he pretended to be just approaching and started to whistle the first tune that popped into his head, "Yankee Doodle", of all things. Nothing happened. No one came to the mouth of the cave to scout out who was there, or to try to make a get-away.

He decided he was being silly, letting his fear and imagination run away. Pushing aside a small bush which hid the low entrance, he crawled into the blackness. Damp, musty air greeted him, but at least it was cool. In time, his eyes adjusted from the intense sunshine outside to the cave's black interior, and he was able to look around. Strange how the space seemed smaller than before. And where were his treasures? His Indian arrow-head and the partridge feather? Gone! There was no sign of the deer skull, either.

Someone must have been in here after all. But who would want to take those things? They weren't worth anything to most people. Only to a young boy. Maybe that was it. Maybe another youngster had discovered "his" cave. Rather than making him angry, the idea felt right. Maybe it was time for him to let go, "to put away childish things", as the good book said. Well, he could live with that. After all, as he'd told Francis Carr just a few weeks ago, he had everything he needed. He could certainly live without an arrow head or a partridge feather.

Rather than the cool comfort he'd anticipated, a chill set in. The cave was damp and musky-smelling. Jamie decided it was time to leave his special place, to go home. As he emerged from the small entrance tunnel and stood up, a blast of humidity greeted him. And something else. She sat in her usual pose, head cocked to one side, intelligent yellow-green eyes surveying him.

"Well, hello," he greeted her. "It's been a while."

He remained still, returning her gaze. Then, the lovely creature advanced slowly, her beautiful, burnished orange tail brushing his legs as lightly as a breath. Pausing to give him one last glance over her shoulder, she entered the cave.

"It's all yours," Jamie said, and with a light heart, he headed for home.

*****

When his cabin came into view, the first thing he noticed was Robbie's wagon parked outside. Something must be up! Nothing bad, he hoped. His father had been fine when he left, but his concern for Melinda caused him to break into a run.

Rushing inside, he found all three, sitting at the table, bright smiles turned toward him. "Well, here he is at last!" Robbie said. "The birthday boy himself!"

His birthday! He hadn't forgotten it, of course, but he'd been sure no one else remembered.

"Happy Birthday, Jamie," Melinda said.

"Thank you," he replied, relieved to see her looking so healthy and well.

"Melinda brought you a cake," Da said. "Can you believe she baked in this heat?"

"Oh, shush! " Melinda looked embarrassed. "It was cool enough early this morning. Besides, Robbie insisted on helping. He beat the eggs!" She beamed with pride.

Robbie actually blushed. "It's no big deal. I didn't think she should be working so hard in this heat. After all, it hasn't been that long since..."

All eyes turned to the sweet infant asleep in the sturdy wooden cradle Ian MacGregor had crafted. On it, he'd carved a tiny MacGregor crest, and below it, her name, *Sarah*. Any suspicions Jamie might have nursed about a MacGregor curse had disappeared with the arrival of this blessing.

"Well, Uncle Jamie," Robbie teased. "How how does it feel to be an old man of seventeen?"

"It feels great!" Jamie beamed with joy, because it did. It felt great to have all his family together again.

"Up the MacGregors!" he cried.

A FAVOUR, PLEASE

If you've enjoyed this story, would you kindly take a moment to rate *MacGregor's Curse* (1-5 stars)

and/or leave a comment at www.goodreads.com

or www.wendytruscott.com

or http://www.facebook.com/hauntedjourney/

Thank you

ACKNOWLEDGEMENT OF TRADITIONAL TERRITORY

For thousands of years Indigenous people have walked in this land, on their own country. Their relationship with the land is at the center of their lives.

We acknowledge the Chippewa, Iroquois and Algonquin People past and present and their stewardship of this land throughout the ages.

*****

THE DISTRICT OF MUSKOKA

Chief Musqua Ukie or Musqua Ukee, also known as Chief William Yellowhead, born about 1769, served with the British during the War of 1812. Named chief of the Deer tribe of the Chippewa (Ojibwa) Indians in 1816, he settled with his band at the site of Orillia, ON, in 1830 in accordance with lieutenant-Governor Colborne's plan for gathering nomadic tribes on reserves. Pressure from white settlers forced the Indians to relinquish their land and Yellowhead's band moved to Rama in 1838- 1839. It is believed that the Muskoka District, which embraced his hunting grounds, was named after this greatly respected chief who died in 1864 and was buried in St. James' churchyard, Orillia, Ontario.

AUTHOR'S NOTES

I am very appreciative of the enthusiastic response my first novel, *Haunted Journey,* received from readers both young and not-so-young. It's especially encouraging for an author to hear from readers who cared enough about her characters to request a sequel..

While a sequel was not my original intention, the idea began to percolate. I felt whatever I wrote next, while satisfying some of those readers' questions, should also be a stand-alone story for those who hadn't yet read *Haunted Journey.* I hope I've accomplished this.

Through the editing process, I concluded there probably is enough useful material for the beginning of a third book, which will still involve some of the current characters, but for the most part will follow Francis on a new adventure which will take him further afield.

While attempting to remain true to conditions in that time period, I realize there may be some errors or omissions, for which I take sole responsibility.

Thank you for taking the time to read this book. I hope you have enjoyed it. Stay tuned for a possible sequel featuring young Francis Carr.

~ Wendy B. Truscott

HAUNTED JOURNEY

"..exciting, historically accurate, and vibrant...Caleb is a loveable, believable character, and the descriptions of Muskoka, people, and the times resonant." - *Dr. Sheila Pennington, PhD. Author of Healing Yourself: Understanding How Your Mind Can Heal Your Body*

"... my nine year old grandson and I have been reading your book together ... and really enjoyed it! I can't believe how many questions it's sparked him to ask me about my childhood. It's really kept his attention and he looks forward to each chapter. In fact he never wants me to stop reading, even when he's exhausted.... It takes a lot to amuse a nine year old so kudos- *Linda Lacroix, CEO Township of Lake of Bays Libraries*

"...a journey into the past of my beloved Canada...to a time when life was kinder and gentler yet harsh and challenging. I was impressed by the author's ability to make pioneer life... come alive. I admired (her) ability to get into the psyche of the various players...especially those in their childhood and teen years... the plot (was) realistic and believable and developed at a pace that truly held my interest."- *John Vellinga*

Read the first chapters of *Haunted Journey* at www.wendytruscott.com   Paperback available on my website. Both paperbacks and e-books available at indigo.com, amazon.com and amazon.ca

ACKNOWLEDGEMENTS

Deep appreciation goes out to so many who have helped bring this novel to fruition. In attempting to list them, no doubt someone will be forgotten, for which I apologize in advance. Every one of you is important to me.

Heartfelt thanks to my friends, the talented members of The Baysville and Bracebridge Library Writing Circles and the Muskoka Authors' Association. Without their constant encouragement and helpful critiques, I would not have had the courage to complete one book, let alone two.

Thank you to the late Melody Richardson, founder of the Writing Circles, for her belief in my abilities and her encouragement to write my first novel, *Haunted Journey*.

Thanks also to the founders of the Muskoka Authors' Association, Cindy Watson, author, *Out of Darkness*, and Wendie Donabie, author and artist, for their continued efforts in arranging speakers and workshops to benefit the many talented writers of this area.

I am indebted to those who have read chapters and offered advice, including: story editor, Ellen Besen; Lori Knowles, co-founder and editor-in-chief, *MuskokaStyle.com;* Sherry Rondeau, author, *Dear Tony, A Caregiver's Journal;* David Bruce Patterson, author, *Square Wheels;* and Judith Watson.

Special thanks to Cheryl Cooper, author of the *Seasons of War* series, for her kind mentoring and encouragement. So many improvements to my manuscript are due to her expert suggestions.

Much appreciation to Shirley Prittie, whose memories of her father's blacksmith shop helped inform this story.

As always, thanks to my amazing husband, for his constant love, encouragement, and support in all my endeavours, and to my children and grandchildren for being the kind, thoughtful, and caring people they are.

ABOUT THE AUTHOR

Wendy B. Truscott learned to love the beauty and history of Muskoka as a child at her family's remote little cottage on a quiet lake. A native of Toronto, ON, she and her husband now live on that same peaceful property. A former teacher, she thrives on creativity, painting, writing, genealogy, reading, and swimming in her beloved lake. Her family inspires her writing and her life.

A member of the Muskoka Authors' Association and the Bracebridge and Baysville Library Writers' Circle, *MacGregor's Curse* is her second novel. She has been published in *Twenty Years*, an anthology of winning poetry from the Northern Ontario Poetry Competition, Muskoka Seniors Magazine, and other local newspapers.

For club, school, or library visits she can be contacted through her website or Facebook.

Follow her on: www.wendytruscott.com and

http://www.facebook.com/hauntedjourney/